$ome

$

M000313364

something blacker than the darkest night.

Antiques dealer (and witch) Cosmo Saville adores
his new husband, but his little white lies—and
some very black magic—are about to bring his
fairytale romance to an end. Someone is killing
San Francisco's spell casters, and the only person
Cosmo can turn to, the man who so recently swore
to love and cherish him, isn't taking his phone calls.

The only magic Police Commissioner John Joseph
Galbraith believes in is true love. Discovering
he's married to a witch—a witch with something
alarmingly like magical powers—is nearly as bad as
discovering the man he loves tricked and deceived
him. John shoulders the pain of betrayal and packs
his bags. But when he learns Cosmo is in the
crosshairs of a mysterious and murderous plot, he
knows he must do everything in his mortal power
to protect him.

Till death do them part. With their relationship on
the rocks, Cosmo and Commissioner Galbraith join
forces to uncover the shadowy figure behind the
deadly conspiracy.

Can the star-crossed couple bring down a killer
before the dark threat extinguishes
true love's flame?

I BURIED A WITCH

Bedknobs and Broomsticks 2

December 2019
Copyright 2019 by Josh Lanyon

Cover by Reese Dante reesedante.com
Cover content is for illustrative purposes only. Any person depicted on the cover is a model.
Editing by Keren Reed
Book design by Kevin Burton Smith
All rights reserved

ISBN: 978-1-945802-95-9

Published in the United States of America
JustJoshin Publishing, Inc.
3053 Rancho Vista Blvd.
Suite 116
Palmdale, CA 93551
www.joshlanyon.com

This is a work of fiction. Any resemblance to persons living or dead is entirely coincidental.

I Buried A Witch

BEDKNOBS AND BROOMSTICKS 2

VELLICHOR BOOKS

An imprint of JustJoshin Publishing, Inc.

To Felice, C.S., and S.C.
When shall we three—er, four—meet again in thunder, lightning, or in rain? Love youse guys.

Double, double, toil and trouble;
Fire burn, and cauldron bubble.

William Shakespeare, *Macbeth*

Chapter One

SCENE I. A CAVERN. IN THE MIDDLE, A BOILING CAULDRON.

Thunder. Enter the three Witches

First Witch

Thrice the brinded cat hath mewed.

Second Wit—

Yeah, totally kidding about that. There was no second witch. It was one witch, me, and John, my husband, SFPD's new police commissioner. Oh, and the scene was the breakfast table at our house on Greenwich Street in San Francisco. I was fixing French toast, which, for the record, is not French, and the coffee was just about ready.

"… new report, you need to make just over $343,000 in order to afford a median-priced home in San Francisco," the bespectacled and solemn news reporter on the TV across the kitchen informed us. "The report was compiled by…"

John and I had arrived home the night before from Scotland, where we had been on our honeymoon for the past two weeks. As a side note, I am very much in favor of honeymoons. I mean, yes, a honeymoon is artificial in that getting to spend two weeks doing whatever pleasurable thing you feel like doing is not real life. And yeah, it's also true that a luxury vacation in a romantic foreign country is probably not the best way to get to know someone you've only known a short time—although it certainly works that way in Hallmark movies. But it *is* a good way to figure out if you want to spend more time together, and needless to say, I had figured out I wanted to spend as much time as possible with John.

Ideally, the rest of my life.

John poured coffee into two mugs. "You're still okay with hosting this cocktail party on Sunday?"

"Of course." He cocked an eyebrow. "What?" I asked.

He nodded at the mountain of cardboard boxes filling half the kitchen. It was pretty much the same situation in every room of the house. Combining our separate households meant John and I had bestowed a lot of worldly goods on each other. And then we'd bought a few new pieces too, like the Victorian black and bronze bed in the master bedroom.

"I've got a lot of catching up to do over the next few days. I'm not going to be able to give you much help. Presumably it's going to be the same for you."

"I can manage. Don't worry. I'll have Bridget."

John looked unconvinced, but he poured a generous helping of cream and sugar into my coffee and brought it to me with a kiss.

"I'm going to miss you today," he murmured.

"Same here." I kissed him back.

That led to another longer kiss, and before I knew it, I was sitting on the quartz counter with my jeans unbuttoned, the French toast was burning, and the doorbell was ringing.

"*Hell*," John exclaimed, hastily tucking his shirt in and zipping up his trousers. "That's Aloha."

"Yes, it is." I sighed. "In more ways than one."

Aloha Newman was John's driver. Though she worked for SFPD, she was not actually a police officer and did not carry a gun. That was fine by me. I'd had more than enough of guns on our wedding day.

What Aloha *did* possess was a ruthless sense of punctuality.

"I'll see you around six." John was already heading for the arched doorway leading into the dining room.

"We're having dinner at your mother's," I called after him.

He muttered something uncomplimentary to the universe, then returned, "Right. See you at five-thirty."

The front door slammed behind him.

I sighed, glanced at the stove, and twitched my nose. The dial turned to off, the flame beneath the pan guttered and died. "*Down the sink, before you stink,*" I muttered.

Two burned slices of egg-coated bread rose from the pan, floated past my face, and dropped down the sink drain.

Across the room, another reporter, also bespectacled and solemn but female, stood in front of an ordinary-looking suburban home cordoned off with crime-scene tape. The reporter was saying, "Though friends of the victim say Ms. Starshine was a practicing Wiccan, investigators speculate these 'Satanic' elements might be intended to divert suspicion from the killer or killers." A photo in the corner of the screen showed a young woman in her mid-thirties with long fair hair and a tentative smile.

"What the what?" I hopped off the counter and went to turn up the sound on the television—the remote was still MIA— which promptly zapped me. "*Ouch!*"

The volume blasted up, then died away again.

By the time I managed to dial in the sound, the cameras had returned to the studio, and the news anchors, recognizable for the lack of spectacles or solemnity, were exchanging cheery banter about the weather forecast. Sunny with a chance of homicide?

I made a mental note to ask John about the Starshine case, turned off the TV, and sprinted upstairs to get changed for work.

*   *   *   *   *

"How was Scotland?" Andi asked when I stopped by her apartment in Alamo Square to pick up Pyewacket.

Andi—Andromeda Merriweather—has been my best friend since I can remember. Her mother and my mother were chums back in the day, and apparently it was a dream come true to be able to share morning sickness and swollen feet with their nearest and dearest. I'm not entirely kidding about the nearest and dearest. By the time I came along, my parents were experiencing a certain lack of conjugal enthusiasm, and Andi's father had crossed over, so Maman and Belinda did rely heavily on each other. Girl Power being a magic that transcends realms.

Anyway, Andi is three months older than me. She's tall and slim with short, inevitably spiky red hair, freckles, and hazel eyes. She owns and operates the Mad Batter bakery, which has The Best cupcakes in all of San Francisco. And I don't say that merely because I concoct the recipes for her exclusive line of cocktail cupcakes.

"Bonnie," I answered, cuddling Pye. Pyewacket is my three-hundred-year-old Familiar. I mean, I haven't had him for three hundred years—I only turned twenty-nine in May. Pye inhabits the body of a cat. A Russian Blue cat.

I kissed Pye's nose, which he bore stoically. "Was he any trouble?" I asked.

Kind of a rhetorical question, but Andi shook her head, smiling as she watched us. "He's good company for Minerva." Minerva is Andi's Familiar, a Dwarf Hotot rabbit with a disposition as benign as the carrots she loves to snack on.

"Did you have fun?" I asked Pye.

His meow was loud and scented with liver-flavored Friskies Paté.

"I bet," I said.

"So, everything is…good?" Andi asked—maybe a little tentatively.

"Everything is great." I guess I was beaming because Andi looked relieved.

"You *look* happy."

"I am. I don't think I've ever been this happy before." To be honest, it was a little unsettling. Obviously, the honeymoon phase couldn't last forever, and I wasn't sure how much of

John's and my contentment with each other was the result of a couple of weeks of nothing to do but sightsee and make love.

"I'm glad."

I didn't doubt it. If anyone had a vested interest in my relationship with John working out, it was Andi, who was, when you thought about it, inadvertently responsible for the whole thing. "How's it going with Trace?" I asked.

"Great."

I hadn't expected that. Andi's, well…picky.

"Really? That's wonderful." At least I hoped so. She didn't look as enthused as "great" seemed to warrant.

"Is it? I mean, I really, *really* do like him." She sounded troubled.

"But that's good, right?"

"No. Not right. I'm not like you. I can't— He's mortal. Being together would mean, well, I'm not even sure what it would mean. A lifetime of living a lie? Or breaking my oath and telling him the truth?"

I considered. "As far as oaths go, don't you think the not-telling-any-mortals-anything-ever rule is really more of a guideline?"

"No. I don't."

"Because some mortals *do* know." I was thinking of Ralph Grindlewood. Not that Ralph was a great example, given that I now believed he was the sworn enemy of the Craft.

"That can't be helped. It doesn't change anything. We *cannot* contribute to their knowledge."

In our silence lies our safety.

The final—and some would say the most important—of the Ten Precepts.

Still, I persisted, "I understand, but times *are* changing. Mortals are more accepting now. Of a lot of things."

"Not really. Fashions change. That's about it. And even fashion cycles around again."

Kind of a bleak outlook from a girl who made cupcakes for a living, but Andi's feelings mirrored those of a lot of our friends—and both of our families.

"Yeah, but even two-steps-forward-one-step-back means progress. Incremental maybe, but progress."

She shook her head. "You're an idealist, Cos."

I let it go and changed the subject. "Well, on the topic of fashion, I brought you something frae Bonnie Scotland." I shifted Pye onto my shoulder and handed over a small box.

Andi took it with a pleased smile. "*Oh.* You didn't have to."

"I know."

She unwrapped the box, lifted the lid, and her face changed. "Oh, *Cos.*" She picked up the necklace inside. A tiny carved cinnabar heart crowned with a raw garnet stone dangled from a vintage bogwood rosary.

"It's *lovely.*"

"I found it in an antiques shop in Dumbarton. It's Wiccan, I think."

"I'm sure it is." The silky living warmth of the wood and the quiet fire lying within the gemstone were a giveaway. "I love it. Thank you."

"And I've been thinking of a Drambuie-based cocktail that might work for cupcakes."

Her eyes lit. "Perfect timing. We need to reboot our menu for autumn."

"Autumn? It's only June."

"Exactly. Time to start planning."

We chatted another minute or two and made plans to meet for lunch on Tuesday. I coaxed Pyewacket into his carrier and headed for the door.

As I was leaving, I asked, "Have you heard anything about Rex?"

Rex was a friend of ours who had been injured in a hit-and-run accident. When John and I had left for Scotland, they had still been in a coma.

Andi shook her head. "Sorry. Nothing. But then I'm not sure I would hear anything. They're really more your friend than mine."

"What about Oliver?"

"Oliver?"

"Oliver Sandhurst."

Andi only looked more confused. "What about him?"

"I thought I told you this. He disappeared after I tried to—after my visit to the Creaky Attic."

"Oh. Right. That feels like a million years ago. I haven't heard anything." She looked apologetic. Not that Oliver was her responsibility. Technically, he wasn't my responsibility either.

But I did fear for him. And I did feel responsible.

Confused yet?

Let's recap. A month ago, I met John Joseph Galbraith, San Francisco's new police commissioner and my husband-to-be, at Bonhams' warehouse, where we were both interested in bidding on a black and bronze Victorian antique four-poster with crystal bedknobs. I was attracted to John from the minute I laid eyes on him. I don't know why exactly, because he wasn't really my type. Not that I think of myself as having a type, but if I did, it wouldn't be a big, brusque Kennedyesque guy with a military background and political ambitions.

Except, somehow, when I gazed into John's amber—yes, brown-gold—eyes, something funny happened to me. I'm not saying it was love at first sight, but I did feel some instant, odd connection. Which is why it sort of smarted that John didn't feel the same. In fact, he was kind of…well, let's say pointedly not interested.

Which, come to think of it, maybe *is* a sign of interest?

Or maybe I'd just like to believe that John caustically brushing me off was the equivalent of Gideon Terwilliker pushing Andi into the swimming pool back when we were in the third grade?

Anyway, Andi did not appreciate that slight to my ego, and she, er…cast a spell on John so that the next time he saw me, he, well, fell in love.

Or thought he did.

Which is sometimes the same thing.

And sometimes not.

That explains John's part in all this. It doesn't explain why I went ahead and married a man I'd only known two weeks. But you know, you either believe in love at first sight or you don't. And if you don't, you're quite right not to, because it will never happen to you.

I don't say that to be unkind. It's a fact. If you can't conceive of a thing, how will you recognize it when it happens? Unless we're talking about an earthquake. But anyway, it's right there in the Bible: *Jesus said unto him, If thou canst believe, all things are possible to him that believeth.*

It does happen to some of us. It happened to me.

Granted, part of what—who—I fell so head-over-heels for was the John under the influence of the love spell. The John *not* under a love spell was a different bloke. Not nearly as romantic—or malleable. Yet it didn't seem to matter to my heart.

Regardless of the bait, once a fish is hooked, it's hooked.

I forgot to mention the part where, a couple of days before our wedding, I was suspected of murdering Seamus Reitherman, a fellow witch in the Abracadantès tradition. I was—patently, since I'd just returned from my honeymoon—exonerated, but unfortunately, the police had arrested the wrong person.

Or at least, that was my theory before I went to Scotland for two weeks.

After two weeks of Scottish history, Scottish weather, Scottish booze, and an encounter with a Scottish ghost (a story for a later date), I was not quite as sure. Scottish women are that rare mix of ruthless pragmatism and blazing idealism. So yeah, it was possible that Ciara Reitherman had killed her husband. She had tried to kill me.

Then again, Ciara's attempts to kill me had almost certainly been driven by her belief that *I'd* killed Seamus.

Or maybe not.

Occam's razor, as John had pointed out when I'd tried to make a case for Ciara being wrongly arrested. The simplest explanation is the most likely. At least when it comes to police work, according to the police commissioner in the family. It was far more likely Ciara had killed her unfaithful (and generally exasperating) husband than that some shadowy global conspiracy tried to frame me for murder.

Not that I had told John about the shadowy global conspiracy that might or might not really exist.

Just one of the things I hadn't told John about.

* * * * *

"Welcome home. We missed you," Blanche greeted me, when I finally arrived at Blue Moon Antiques, cat carrier and peevish occupant in tow.

"Thank you. It's good to be home." I gazed with satisfaction around the spacious and airy downstairs showroom. Light streaming through the protectively tinted bay windows glanced off gilt curlicues and silvered glass, warmed the velvets and brocades of aged upholstery, glinted off ivory scrimshaw and ebony trinket boxes. The air was infused with beeswax and carnuba. The scent of history—and secrets.

Blanche asked, "How's married life?"

"I *highly* recommend it."

Blanche Baker has been working for me since I opened Blue Moon Antiques four years ago. The customers love her. I love her. In fact, everyone loves Blanche. She's about fifty. Tall and voluptuous with black, curly hair—currently streaked with indigo—and one blue eye and one green eye behind a seemingly infinite wardrobe of rhinestone glasses (I'm partial to the ones with butterfly-shaped frames). Her makeup is on the sexy-witch side, but she's not a witch. She's Wicca. Like most mortals, she's not aware there's a difference.

Blanche chuckled, said cheerfully, "No thank you. I've been inoculated against *that* disease. Twice."

"So then you're a carrier?"

"Ha." She took the cat carrier from me, set it on the counter, and lifted Pyewacket out. "Oh, you beautiful baby, what has he *done* to you?"

Pyewacket proceeded to detail his list of grievances into her sympathetic ear.

"Don't listen to him," I said. "He's been living it up on catnip and dried shrimp at Andi's." I glanced around the still empty shop. "Where's Ambrose?"

Blanche sighed. "Another problem with his grandma."

"Another what problem?"

"I don't know. He's being very closemouthed about it."

My good mood deflated a fraction. "How long has this been going on?"

"Not long. The Tuesday after you left, he had to leave suddenly, but he was back the next day, and he's been here every day since. Until this morning. There's a message on the machine. The poor kid is clearly stressed out of his mind."

"Okay. I'll deal with it."

I had hired Ambrose right before the wedding. He'd been recommended by the previously mentioned Ralph Grindlewood. Ralph was a good customer and, once I'd have said, a friend. What exactly Ralph was now, I wasn't sure. But I had hired Ambrose and agreed to make him my apprentice, so *he* was most definitely my concern.

"Anything else I should know before I start going through my mail?"

Blanche, still coddling Pyewacket, shook her head. "It's actually been very quiet since you left."

"Well, we'll see what I can do to change that."

She chuckled. "I don't doubt it."

All the same, she looked pretty surprised when she poked her head into my office a few minutes later to whisper, "Pierre Sjoberg is here to see you."

I put down the catalog for Alexanders Auctioneers. "Who?" The name was vaguely familiar, but I couldn't quite place it.

"The defense attorney." Blanche was still whispering. She threw a quick, uneasy glance over her shoulder as though she feared Sjoberg was lurking behind her. "I think he's *her* attorney."

"Her—?"

Blanche hissed, "*Ciara.* Ciara Reitherman. The woman who tried to kill you!"

Chapter Two

Oh, right. *That* her.

Not that they were lining up—I hoped—but I'd been kind of preoccupied since the last time an attempt on my life had been made.

"I see," I said slowly, although I really didn't. "Send him in, then?"

Blanche nodded, ducked out, and opened the door a moment or two later for a short, bald, dapperly dressed man of about sixty.

"Pierre Sjoberg," Blanche announced, and promptly closed my office door.

Sjoberg said heartily, "Cosmo Saville, Duc of Westlands. This is an honor, Your Grace."

I rose to shake his hand, saying hastily, "I don't really do the *duc* thing, if you don't mind. It's just Mr. Saville."

His hand was soft and smooth, but he had a grip like a professional wrestler. "Mr. Saville, then. Forgive the intrusion. I'm sure you're buried, after your honeymoon, but it's rather urgent that I speak to you."

"All right," I said, still dubious. "Please sit down."

Sjoberg drew up an Erwin-Lambeth plum velvet Neo-Chippendale wing chair and sat down. He clasped his hands over his trim midsection and smiled at me from across the mail-strewn desk.

"I don't know if you're aware that I'm representing Ciara Reitherman in the homicide of Seamus Reitherman."

I said tartly, "And the attempted homicide of me? No, I wasn't aware."

Sjoberg looked pained. "My client deeply regrets her actions. She was beside herself with grief. In fact, that's why I'm here. Ciara would like to speak with you and personally convey her remorse. Among other things."

"Uh, that's okay," I said. "No meeting necessary. I'll take your word for it."

"I understand your reluctance, but my client has given her oath that she will attempt no further harm to you by methods natural or supernatural. Harm to you is the last thing she would wish. Ciara needs your help. She's innocent of the charges laid against her."

"She's not innocent of trying to kill me. I was there when it happened, and there's no doubt in my mind. She wanted me— and probably anyone who got in her way—dead."

"She doesn't deny it." Sjoberg actually waved his hand in dismissal. "At that moment in time she was, as I said, not herself. *Non compos mentis*. No, the charge I'm specifically referring to is the homicide of Seamus Reitherman."

"Hm."

As mentioned, I already suspected Ciara had not killed Seamus. Surely the proof of that was in her unrelenting attempts to avenge him by killing *me*.

That is not to say all was forgiven. See above. It's one thing when family tries to kill you. Murder attempts from casual social acquaintances? Not cool.

I was curious, though.

"And this would be of interest to me because…?"

"Because Seamus Reitherman was Abracadantès, and one day you will take the reins of that tradition."

I said shortly, "*Should* that day arrive, it'll be a long time coming."

"Even so," Sjoberg replied.

Goddess help any tradition I was reigning over. Still, I saw his point. Not that I agreed, necessarily, but I did owe Seamus something for sending the *Grimorium Primus* to me. Or rather, to *Société du Sortilège*. In the end, his loyalty to the Abracadantès had outweighed his self-interest—and so it was with me as well.

"What exactly does Ciara want me to do?"

He hesitated, and it occurred to me that he was not exactly sure himself. "Other than pledging no harm to you, she hasn't confided in me. Presumably, she'll relay that information when—if—you meet with her."

"I see." I really didn't.

Sjoberg said with sudden and convincing sincerity, "I believe her. I believe she's innocent, and I have more than a little experience in judging whether people are telling me the truth. She's desperate to speak to you. I think she does regret attempting to harm you, but it's more than that."

Now *that*, I didn't doubt.

I wasn't sure I trusted Ciara's promise of no harm, but I did trust that her plight was dire enough that she wouldn't jeopardize whatever she hoped to gain from our meeting. Plus, forewarned is forearmed. The last time, I'd been unprepared and otherwise occupied. This time I'd be on guard.

I said at last, "All right. I'll speak to her. Is she out on bail?"

"Of course not." The silver triangles of Sjoberg's eyebrows rose at my ignorance of how such things worked. "After attempting to kill the police commissioner's husband? Bail will not be an option. No, you'll have to visit her in County Jail #2 either tomorrow or Sunday."

Not exactly convenient. "Why tomorrow or Sunday?"

Sjoberg said patiently, "That's when visiting hours are."

"Oh. Right. Well, it'll have to be tomorrow, then." At least it wouldn't inconvenience John since he'd be working most of the weekend in an effort to get caught up. Still, it was liable to be awkward.

"I'll see that you're added to the list."

"Thank you," I said, though I wasn't feeling particularly thankful.

I was still sorting through mail, still sorting through possible reasons Ciara might need to see me, when Ambrose knocked on the doorframe.

"I'm here," he said. "Sorry I'm late." His dark eyes flicked to mine, flicked away.

"Come in," I invited. "Shut the door and pull up a pew."

He entered reluctantly and took the chair so recently vacated by Pierre Sjoberg. He hunched forward, bony hands gripping his knees.

Ambrose Jones, my newest hire and first apprentice witchling, was a tall and slight twenty-one-year-old with a mop of wild dark hair and eyes as wide and black as those Big Eyes paintings by Margaret Keane.

"What's going on?" I asked.

Ambrose's gaze found mine. His expression was blank.

"Why were you late?"

He looked ever so slightly affronted. "I just *was*."

Once upon a time, not that long ago, I was twenty-one too. I remembered how it worked. "Blanche said something happened with your grandmother?"

Something odd, almost like fear, flashed through his eyes. "It's nothing to do with GramMa."

I tilted my head, asked curiously, "What is it to do with?"

He licked his lips, said, "It's just...I was upset. About Abby. I used to... We were... We used to be friends."

"Abby?"

"Abby Starshine. She was—" His Adam's apple jumped as he gulped. "Murdered. I just found out this morning. It was on the news."

Ms. Starshine. Yes. I remembered there had been a news story about a slain Wiccan. Remembered something about the newscaster saying the crime had Satanic elements. I'd intended to ask John about it, although I'd forgotten that until now.

I said automatically, "Blessed is the Circle of Life. Blessed is our journey through sunshine and shadow." Studying his face, I added, "I'm so sorry, Ambrose. To lose someone to violence is a great shock."

He nodded, again avoiding my gaze. That worried me. Ambrose had always struck me as shy but direct. Then again, I didn't really know him. I'd left for my honeymoon right after hiring him.

"Were you still—"

"I haven't seen her for months," he interrupted.

"Okay. Right." Something was wrong here, but I wasn't sure what, let alone how to address it. "I guess that makes it more difficult?"

He did meet my gaze then. "It's nothing like that, Cosmo. It was all over between us. It was just… You said it yourself—it's a shock to hear that she's…crossed."

"Yes, of course."

"There wasn't *anything* still there. I mean, there weren't *bad* feelings. There weren't *any* feelings."

"Um, sure." The more he talked, the less I believed him.

"Anyway." Ambrose rose. "Was there anything else?"

I leaned back and considered him. "Well, yes. There is. We should probably discuss your apprenticeship."

He sank back onto the purple cushions, staring at me. "Are you— Am I— Are you going to take me for your apprentice?"

"Yes."

"But…why?"

I gave a short laugh. He seemed more shocked than pleased. "I thought that was the idea. Don't you want me to?"

Something blazed in the back of his eyes. "*Yes.* More than anything. But I thought… I didn't think you would."

I shrugged. I didn't want to go into my reasons for changing my mind. Not yet. Ambrose's life seemed complicated enough, at least from the outside. The news that he might be a potential pawn in a war between the Craft and a secret organization known as the Society for Prevention of Magic in the Mortal Realm might freak him out.

It kind of freaked *me* out.

"Talent without training is useless," I said. "And in our case, it's dangerous."

He nodded doubtfully, but at least some healthy color finally suffused his face. "When will we start?"

"Now. I want you to begin assembling your grimoire."

"A *grimoire*?" Some of the light went out of his eyes. "But that's…"

"What?"

"Isn't that for old ladies?"

"I beg your pardon?"

He reddened. "I just mean, well, *these* days isn't that for Wiccans and…and *old* witches?"

"Of course not."

Ambrose looked unconvinced.

I repeated firmly, "Of course not. A grimoire is an absolute necessity for a practicing witch. Why on earth would you think putting together your own personal book of spells and incantations is something obsolete?"

How did he imagine modern witches cast spells? Through text?

Come to think of it…after Seamus's murder I *had* received some peculiar text messages. Not every witch had my precarious relationship with technology.

Ambrose raised his chin. "Isn't it? What does any textbook have to do with real life?"

"*What?* First of all, Gardner's *Book of Shadows* is a textbook. The *Lesser Key of Solomon* is a textbook. *Your* grimoire isn't a textbook. It's the map of your journey through your life in the Craft."

His lip curled. "That's worse. In other words, it's scrapbooking."

This is why I never wanted to teach. Teaching is an art. It requires patience. It requires perseverance. Did I mention it requires patience? Anyway, it's an art I do not possess.

"You know what? Maybe it is. Maybe it's part scrapbook, part recipe book, part *Thomas Guide*, and…I don't know. Part family Bible. You can think of it however you like. The point is, you need to begin compiling yours ASAP. I started mine when I was eight, so you've got some catching up to do."

He rolled his eyes. "What does any book have to do with real power?"

I said menacingly, "You've worked in bookstores for how many years? And you ask me this?"

Ambrose's expression was sheepish but stubborn. "You know what I mean."

"Nope. I certainly do not."

"But how do I even begin? The whole reason I need you is I don't know any real spells."

I laughed. "The fact that you think *that's* what you need me for is proof of how much you need me."

He looked confused—and fair enough.

I had a flash of inspiration. "Have you ever heard of the Miyagi tradition?"

"No."

"Good. We're going to begin your training using some of the time-honored Miyagi methods. One week from today I want to see your grimoire."

Ambrose opened his mouth, met my gaze, closed it. He nodded.

"Good. You can go." I pointed at the door and returned to flipping through auction catalogs.

Ambrose rose and headed for the door. Hand on the knob, he stopped and turned back. He said casually—too casually, "Cosmo, do you think the police will want to talk to me?"

I could see the anxiety he was trying to hide beneath his stoic expression, and my heart sank.

"If you haven't seen Abby for months, I can't see why they would. I don't know, though. I guess it depends on how things ended between you."

I was hoping to hear something reassuring. Instead, Ambrose nodded, opened the door, and went out.

First thing I did was phone my mother.

I should probably clarify. I mean, I'm fond of *ma mère*, certainly, but it was in her role as Duchesse d'Abracadantès, the witch first in line for accession to the seat of the Crone that I needed to talk to her. If anyone would have a handle on current events related to Witch World, it was she.

(By the way, no one calls the Craft *Witch World*. That's my little joke. I loved those Andre Norton books when I was a kid.)

Anyway, per her vapid companion Phelon Penn, *Maman* was out of the country.

"Where is she?" I asked.

"Paris," Phelon replied.

"Why is she in Paris?" It was galling to have to ask, but my mother does not possess a cell phone. Not, like me, because her relationship with technology is dicey. In Maman's case, it's because she rejects the entire concept of cell phones as rude, inelegant, and intrusive.

Phelon, who thinks as highly of me as I do of him, replied, "You'll have to ask her," and hung up.

Paris was the seat of the *Société du Sortilège*, but it was also where my mother, still *citoyen français*, preferred to shop, so maybe there was a weighty reason behind her sudden trip abroad or maybe she was out of real Dijon mustard.

Hopefully, if she phoned home—though why would anyone wish to speak to Phelon if they didn't have to?—her companion would tell her I'd phoned. But I wouldn't bet on it.

So next I called John at City Hall.

Or rather, I called his executive assistant, Pat Anderson. Pat is an efficient, charming, and capable woman, which means she's very good at reassuring me I'm the person John most wants to speak to even as she relegates me to the back of the queue.

Which I totally get.

Obviously, the mayor, the police chief, the assistant chiefs, and the deputy chiefs take precedence. Then comes me. Usually. If there's a crisis in the city, the phone tree branches above my own perch include the commanders, the executive director, and even, potentially, the directors.

It appeared there *was* a crisis in progress because after asking all the right things about Scotland and the new house, Pat apologetically informed me that John was on a conference call and was going to be a while.

"That's all right," I said, trying to be a good sport. "It wasn't anything that can't wait." Besides, now that I'd had time to think, I realized I needed to do a little research of my own before broaching the subject of a murdered Wiccan with John.

"I know there's no voice he'd rather hear," Pat said, which was sweet but probably not at all true. John was not particularly romantic.

Which was fine because it turned out I was romantic enough for both of us.

Anyway, I thanked Pat and clicked off.

I was Googling Abigail Starshine a short time later when my cell phone rang. My sister-in-law Jinx's photo popped up, and I pressed to accept.

I was smiling as I answered, "Hey, stranger."

"How was Scotland? Are you going to request an annulment?"

I snorted. "Certainly not. And Scotland was brilliant."

"Did John buy a kilt?"

"Um, yes."

She laughed. "Did you buy a kilt?"

"Um, no."

She laughed again. We chatted for a bit, and then she said, "Remember when I asked if you'd like to meet my coven's Witch Queen?"

I stopped smiling. Wiccans, mortals, and even different Craft traditions use the term *Witch Queen* to mean a variety of things. Even so, it's not a title given or taken on lightly. I had never heard of Valenti Garibaldi, the Witch Queen in question, before the night of my stag party when Jinx had informed me she was part of Garibaldi's coven.

That news was not in itself alarming. Or at least, not alarming to me. I didn't think Jinx was a witch, but it's not always possible to tell. She thought she was a witch. And it seemed Valenti Garibaldi thought Jinx was a witch.

Garibaldi probably *was* a witch. I had sensed it the first time I saw her.

What else she might be, I was unsure, but I thought there was a pretty good chance murderess might be among the possibilities. Accomplice might be best-case scenario. Any scenario was liable to spell disaster for John.

I said, "I remember."

"I asked Valenti about it, and she would like to meet you. Formally meet you, I mean. I know you sort of met at the wedding."

"Yes."

"So are you still interested?"

Oh yes. I was still interested.

"When and where?"

"Now," Jinx said. "She's invited us to have lunch."

Chapter Three

"I've never been to Scotland," Valenti Garibaldi was saying. "But from what I understand, nearly the entire country is one great vortex of arcane power."

"Certainly since Brexit," I said.

Valenti smiled, her sea-glass-colored eyes chilly as the equatorial cold tongue. Jinx kicked my ankle. Before I could correct my course, the waiter appeared to take our orders.

We were lunching at Spruce in Pacific Heights.

I'd dined there a few times, but only for dinner. In fact, it's famous for being the place where the newly liberated bring their parents for that first meal to celebrate financial independence. The dining room offered cathedral-style ceilings and a skylight, the lighting warm and shadowy, and the modern decor leaned toward urban masculine with tonal accents of leather and tobacco. It did not seem like a natural setting for Valenti, but maybe she just really appreciated a good bar and an excellent menu, both of which Spruce possessed.

John would have loved the wine list. I ordered another Modern—blended scotch whisky, sloe gin, lemon, Regan bitters, and absinthe—and the cheeseburger. It's not true about Scottish cuisine being bland and boring, but if you want a hamburger, a *real* hamburger—and I'd been craving one for the last week—you have to get it in the States.

Jinx said, "My mother's very into genealogy. I don't care about that stuff. I guess John does."

John's interest in his Scottish heritage seemed to spring from his taking one of those DIY DNA tests. I found his interest in the results more interesting than the results themselves, but then my own family heritage had been discussed ad nauseum from my earliest childhood.

Valenti said, "Scotland has a dark reputation when it comes to its treatment of our kind."

Well, yeah. There was The Great Scottish Witch Hunt of 1590, The Great Scottish Witch Hunt of 1597, The Great Scottish Witch Hunt of 1628, The Great Scottish Witch Hunt of 1649, and, finally, The Great Scottish Witch Hunt of 1661. All told, anywhere from four to six thousand people—not all of them witches, by any means—lost their lives during this particular Scottish pastime.

I said, "It was John's first trip, so we pretty much stuck to the beaten path. We did the Festival of Wine in Glasgow, the Riverside Museum, the Kelvingrove Art Gallery and Museum. Mostly we did a lot of walking and drinking and talking."

"Suuuuuure," Jinx said.

I gave her my most discouraging look. She grinned.

Valenti said thoughtfully, "There's an extensive collection of books relating to the history of witchcraft and demonology at the University of Glasgow, isn't there?"

"The Damned Art exhibition," I agreed. Given the Society for Prevention of Magic in the Mortal Realm's mission, I wondered if this was a casual question or if the collection had been targeted.

In fairness, I didn't know for sure that Valenti was a member of SPMMR. I assumed she was because of her connection to Ralph. But as I knew better than anyone, bedfellows make for strange politics.

Speak of the devil. My cell phone rang, and John's photo, taken on a rare sunny day on Glas Maol, flashed up. My heart rose. "Excuse me," I said. "I need to take this."

I left the table and made my way to the foyer. "Hey."

"Hey," John said. "Pat said you phoned earlier."

"I did. It wasn't anything important. Mostly I just wanted to hear your voice."

He made a sound that fell somewhere between a snort and a smile. "I miss you too. Are you having a good day?"

"Sure. As a matter of fact, I'm having lunch with Jinx and her friend Valenti." I was curious whether Valenti's name would ring a bell with him.

"Are you? What's Jinx up to?"

To start with, she thinks she's a witch, and she wanted me to meet her coven's Witch Queen, who I think might be involved with Rex's hit-and-run accident.

Can you imagine if I'd said that aloud?

But really, in a perfect world, I *could* have said it out loud. In a perfect world, I would have been able to tell John the truth about myself, and I'd have been able to warn him that I thought Jinx might be wading into deep and dangerous waters.

As it was, I said vaguely, "You know Jinx."

"Yes, I do," John said grimly. "Don't let her monopolize your afternoon."

"No, I won't."

"Was there anything else?" he asked.

I thought of Ambrose and Abigail Starshine, but that wasn't something to bring up during a hurried phone call. "No. Just…I love you."

He made that little sound again, said softly, "I love you too. I'll see you this evening."

Then he waited for me to click off, which I did without further delay.

Back at the table, I could see Valenti speaking quietly and Jinx nodding, her expression unhappy. I resolved to make a better impression on the local Witch Queen.

"Sorry about that," I said, taking my seat at the table.

Our meals had arrived in the interim. After the sad fate of my breakfast, I was starving, and I dived right in. Valenti and

Jinx nibbled at their salads and made cryptic small talk. Jinx usually eats like a horse, so I assumed it was the presence of the Witch Queen putting her off her feed.

Finally, Valenti put down her wineglass and said, "Cosmo, Jinx tells me you share her interest in witchcraft. You wear the sacred symbols on your bracelet and a witch's amulet around your neck. Do you belong to a coven?"

I hesitated. She was Ralph Grindlewood's friend—in fact, I'd taken it for granted she was his girlfriend—so surely, she knew everything Ralph did about me? And Ralph knew far too much. Knew that I was Craft. Knew that there was such a thing as Craft. Maybe I should have anticipated the question—and this line of discussion—but for some reason I'd imagined we would mostly talk about Jinx. Or, better yet, about Valenti. I had *wanted* to talk about Valenti.

"Not now," I replied.

"But you've been a member of the sacred circle in the past." It was not a question.

Jinx watched us attentively, and I felt a flash of unease. Jinx did not know of Craft. Was Valenti so lost to propriety, to commonsense, she might reveal the truth to a mortal?

If Jinx learned the truth, it would not be long before John also knew it. That I was quite sure of.

"Yes. When I was younger."

Valenti smiled. I understood that smile, at least partly. I understood that my decision not to lie confirmed something for her. And I saw that I was right. She knew *exactly* what I was—and not surprising, but still worrying, *who* I was.

"Perhaps you feel your brothers and sisters failed you?"

"No, I wouldn't say that. Not at all."

She said softly, "Perhaps you failed them?"

That was not a question I expected. It took me aback. "I don't think so. I hope not."

She appeared to think it over. "Perhaps you're someone who prefers to study and practice in solitude?"

"Perhaps."

"For our kind, safety lies in numbers."

Jinx said eagerly, "*Exactly.*"

"Not always."

Valenti shrugged her slim shoulders and said, "There's no rule without exception. But barring betrayal, we're all stronger together."

Joined hands are the strongest. It's the sixth Precept.

Also commonsense.

"Are you inviting me to join one of your covens?"

Jinx's breath caught as though in hope. Valenti glanced at her and shook her head.

"Not at this time, sadly. I think however much you would benefit from the discipline and structure of the sacred circle, you are not there yet. Our novitiates must be willing to forget all previous training, must assume an attitude of humility and servitude, and finally, must be willing to accept the word of their High Priestess as law in all things. Do you think you're at that place spiritually, emotionally, and intellectually?"

I said, "Pretty doubtful."

Or, *hell to the no.* As the mortals say.

Jinx said, dismayed, "Oh, *Cos.*"

Valenti's lip lifted in a slightly scornful smile. "I suspect you may regret your attitude in the not-too-distant future. There's a lot I could teach you. A lot you don't know."

I shrugged. "Well, that's what they say: never stop learning because life never stops teaching."

This conversation was confusing for a number of reasons. If Ralph Grindlewood was, as I believed, a member—maybe a leader—in the Society for Prevention of Magic in the Mortal Realm, and Valenti was in cahoots with him, *why* would she be recruiting members for her coven? Why did she even *have* a coven?

And that's what this felt like. An interview.

An interview I had apparently failed.

Valenti was Craft. Well, a witch. Without tradition? Self-taught? Perhaps starting her own tradition?

I said, "How long have you known Ralph?"

"A little over a year. We were both customers of Seamus Reitherman. I managed to grab a wonderful vintage scrying mirror before Ralph could get his hands on it."

"The Creaky Attic," Jinx said. "I loved that place. It's such a shame what happened. I wonder if Mrs. Reitherman will be convicted."

"I hope not," I said. "She's innocent."

"*Innocent?*" Jinx looked astonished. "But she's not innocent. She tried to kill you."

"Er, yes. But anyone can make a mistake."

Valenti said, "So true." Her pale-green gaze held mine for a moment. She smiled.

I smiled too. "Who wants dessert?" I asked. "The beignets here are the best I've had outside Paris."

"Not me," Jinx said. "I've got a hair appointment."

I looked at Valenti, who was still smiling, though her eyes were hard and bright. I didn't think she was disappointed. I thought I had confirmed something for her. She said, "No thank you. I don't care for sweets."

"Ah. Well, that's probably for the best. I really should be getting back, but this has been a treat."

There was the usual little back and forth over the bill, which Valenti won—I couldn't fault her determination. I thanked her again for lunch, and then Jinx and I rose to leave.

"I think I'll stay and have a drink at the bar," Valenti said, and we said our goodbyes.

As we were making our way to the front entrance, Jinx hissed, "Why were you acting like that?"

"Like how?"

"Like the-the Comte Comes to Town. You were so arrogant. She's trying to help you. You acted like no one could teach you anything."

"I certainly don't think that."

"You certainly did *act* like you think that." She added, "Why didn't you tell me you used to belong to a coven?"

"Because I don't anymore. It was a long time ago."

Jinx sounded a little aggrieved as she said, "I thought you two would get along so well. You were almost *rude*."

"I'm sorry. I didn't mean to be."

"Yes, but I think you did."

Maybe. I was biased, true enough. I had arrived at this meeting with a full set of preconceptions. None of which had been particularly shaken. I remained skeptical of Valenti's motivations, especially as they regarded Jinx. Jinx's growing disaffection toward her family made her, in my opinion, vulnerable.

I said, "How exactly did you meet Valenti?"

Jinx said vaguely, "Through friends."

I weighed my words. "The thing is, because of your relationship to John, it's possible that some people might—"

"Want to use me?" she said with uncharacteristic dryness.

"Yes."

"I'm not stupid, Cos."

"I know you're not stupid." I also knew that if I kept talking, I was going to make it worse. I said instead, "You know, John can't know about any of this."

"You don't have to tell me," Jinx muttered.

It should have been reassuring, but I didn't want to have to keep secrets from John, let alone secrets that concerned his sister. Nor did I want to encourage Jinx to keep secrets from him.

Jinx edged past a tall man with sun-streaked brown hair and a pleasantly lopsided smile. I smiled back. He did a double take, and said, "Hey, it's you!"

"Is it?" I said warily. I didn't recognize him.

Or did I? There was something familiar about him…

He offered his hand, and we shook. "Cosmo, right? It's me. Chris. Chris Huntingdon."

"Right. Chris." I must have sounded as doubtful as I felt because Chris laughed.

"I guess I'm not surprised. We met at your stag party."

"Oh. *Chris.*" That had been a long and emotional night, but I vaguely remembered dancing with a cute guy in fashionable camo at Misdirections. "I remember."

"We danced all night. I kept trying to get your phone number."

"Did you?" At the time he hadn't seemed unduly persistent. We'd all been dancing—and drinking.

"So…it looks like you did get married?" He glanced at the ring on my left hand and grimaced.

"Yep. I did." I thought I understood why I'd kept dancing with him that night. There was something engaging about him; that mix of unabashed flattery and rueful good humor.

Chris shook his head. "Just my luck."

"Thanks. It was nice seeing you again."

His eyes warmed. "Like fate?"

"Uh…"

"You know what? This is probably not good manners, but." He reached into his wallet and pulled out a card. "If you ever want to go out for drinks or have coffee. No pressure. No hanky-panky. Just friends."

I took the card automatically. "Thanks, but really, I couldn't."

Chris repeated, "Just friends. Not looking for trouble." He nodded pleasantly, nodded again at Jinx, and continued into the main dining room.

"Wow. I call bullshit," Jinx said. "No hanky-panky my eye. You're *married.*"

"I do still get together with friends." I was amused.

"Yeah, but he's *not* a friend. You just met him."

"True." Amused or not, I agreed with her. It was one thing to continue to socialize with existing friends. It was another to start a relationship with someone who had made no secret of being romantically interested.

"You can laugh, but John wouldn't find it funny," Jinx said.

I looked at her in surprise. "Is John the jealous type?"

Jinx seemed to consider. She shrugged. "Isn't everyone?"

We parted ways outside the restaurant. Jinx took an Uber, and I found a postern behind an apartment on Sacramento Street. When I arrived back at Blue Moon, I learned Ambrose had left early.

"Now what's the excuse?" I asked.

"He was very apologetic," Blanche said. She seemed apologetic too, by which I deduced she'd told him he could leave.

"Glad to hear it. Though it doesn't really solve the problem of his not being here when we need him."

"We're not that busy today."

I gave Blanche a look, and she said, "We're not, Cos. I can manage if you want to leave early. I know you're exhausted after that flight."

"It's not that. We're having dinner with John's mother."

"All the more reason to rest up."

I swallowed a laugh and said gravely, "I'll pretend I didn't hear that."

"By their deeds shall they be known," Blanche retorted.

"But what was the kid's excuse?" I persisted. "Is it his grandmother again?"

"He didn't say."

I expelled a long, exasperated breath. However, I *was* tired, and I had a ton of things to do before Sunday's party—especially if I was going to do them without the aid of Craft—so I let Blanche persuade me to leave early.

I bundled Pye into his carrier, summoned an Uber, and returned to the house on Greenwich, where I found Bridget O'Leary waiting in the vestibule. She was a medium-sized woman of indeterminate age with mousy hair tied in an unfashionable bun.

"Sorry I'm late." I put down the carrier and fumbled around for the key to the front door.

Pye purred hello to Bridget, who murmured, "Aren't you the handsome fellow?" To me, she said, "No need to worry, sir. I have my thoughts to keep me company." Her voice was smooth as Irish cream with just a hint of a lilt.

Bridget came recommended to us by John's mother. Apparently, they had become friends at church, and knowing we needed a housekeeper, Nola suggested Bridget. What Nola did not know, of course, was that Bridget was a witch.

I had my own ideas about that. I thought it most likely Maman's was the real hand working the strings in this little domestic puppet show. She would find it doubly amusing for her spy to arrive via Nola.

At last I found my key, opened the door, and beckoned Bridget inside.

"As you can see, we haven't made any real progress since you interviewed."

That was an understatement. In fact, we'd received a ton more boxes and furniture since Bridget had interviewed, and most of it was still sitting in the front room.

She said placidly, "That's why I'm here, sir. Where would you like me to start?"

"If you could tackle the kitchen, that would be a huge help. I still can't find the blender." I lifted Pye out of his carrier.

"Consider it done," Bridget said.

I heard out Pyewacket's complaints. "*Ssst-ssst-ssst.*" I absently stroked his fur, listening to Bridget opening and closing cupboards. I *hoped* Maman had sent her. Otherwise…

Perhaps Pye had the same idea. He leaped from my arms and disappeared into the kitchen.

I turned on the stereo, put on Stevie Nicks' *Bella Donna*, and proceeded to distribute throughout the house the wedding gifts John and I had opened the night before.

It's the thought that counts when it comes to gifts, but I couldn't help wondering if all of John's friends were deranged. The giant painting of a wine cork went straight to John's wet bar. Ditto the unicorn wine-bottle holder. The emergency survival kit (this too a gift from John's military buddies) went into the downstairs guest bathroom.

I carried bundles of assorted linens and towels into the laundry room—checking momentarily when I passed the kitchen doorway and heard Bridget crooning softly to "Edge of Seventeen."

I lugged upstairs a surprisingly heavy green brocade bedspread from Great-aunt Coralie, and put it in the second guest bedroom. My Great-great-great-uncle Arnold, imprisoned in the Louis XVI rococo mirror hanging in the hallway, jabbed his finger at me as he attempted to cast a spell.

I scowled. "You know, if you're not happy here, there's always the Salvation Army."

Uncle Arnold continued to communicate his displeasure, resorting to sign language.

The mirror should be safely out of the way in this part of the house. I just hoped none of our guests were of a snooping disposition. Or if they were, I hoped they confined their nosiness to our medicine cabinets.

"Will you be needing me on Sunday?" Bridget asked when I carried the second compact air fryer into the kitchen.

I tried not to notice that not only were most of the cardboard boxes empty, the containers themselves had been flattened and stacked neatly as if a giant iron had pressed them into shape. The wide marble counters gleamed, comfortably crowded with our new appliances. Neatly stacked china glowed lustrously in the white glass-fronted cupboards. From the white distressed brick of the backsplash to the vintage verdigris dragonfly drawer pulls, everything was magazine-perfect. Nothing out of place and not a smudge nor speck anywhere to be seen.

"Hm? I thought you didn't work on the Sabbath?"

Her smile was as prim and tight as a nun's coif. "I suppose I could be making an exception if you and the commissioner needed me."

My gaze traveled back to the stainless—literally stainless—steel appliances. Bridget had to know that even I, legendary for my nonexistent housekeeping skills, was aware no mortal could manage this in the space of a few hours. Or even a few days.

"It would be helpful, of course, but we wouldn't want to pressure you into doing anything you're uncomfortable with."

She ignored that. "Were you planning to do the cooking yourself?"

"I think so. It's a cocktail party, so we're not serving dinner. Just a few hors d'oeuvres. Nothing too fancy."

"What were you thinking of?"

"Caviar and crème-fraîche tartlets? Shrimp toasts, and mushroom-parmesan palmiers. Easy and quick but elegant."

She looked approving. "I make a very fine lobster toast with avocado."

I looked at her in surprise. "Do you? Well, I could certainly use a hand in the kitchen."

Bridget smiled. Over her shoulder, I saw a sponge in the sink jump up like a happy fish.

Chapter Four

I've always considered the whole Monster-in-Law thing such a tiresome cliché, so imagine my chagrin when my own mother-in-law turned out to be...Nola.

In fairness, Nola had not had it easy. Her first husband, John's father, had died suddenly when John was still very small. It had been up to Nola to support herself and her child. Her second husband, Jinx's father, had died while in bed with Nola's next-door neighbor.

So I was sympathetic to Nola—or at least I wanted to be. Her barely disguised antipathy made it difficult. John assured me it was not personal, but I kind of thought it was.

And even if it wasn't, it wasn't pleasant being on the receiving end of all that pained distaste.

"Are we supposed to have dinner with her every Friday?" I asked casually on the drive over that evening.

John's mouth twitched. "Having second thoughts?"

"No, no!" I said with false heartiness. "Not at all! I can think of no better way to spend our every Friday night!" I was pretending I was kidding, of course, pretending I wasn't really as horrified as I actually was.

John grinned. "Don't worry. It's only once a month, and you don't have to come every time. I can go on my own."

"I don't know about every month, but I'll come most of the time."

"You're a very sweet guy, Cos." He sounded almost surprised.

"I am," I agreed. "I hope you remember that when we have our first argument."

He reached for my hand, folding it lightly, warmly, in his own. "Didn't we already do that?"

"If we did, it can't have been too important. I don't remember it."

He smiled and gave my hand a squeeze.

* * * * *

I'd only been to Nola's home once before—the afternoon John and I went there to tell her we were engaged.

I didn't remember much about the house, but I knew that after he got out of the service, John had purchased the two-bedroom modern farmhouse in the suburb of Larkspur for her. It was a nice little place, and it had been completely ungraded with new carpet and fresh paint and granite counters. It had a sun porch and a deck, and was located in a 55+ park, complete with club house and salt-water pool, which Nola made a point of telling John she never used.

Everything was as neat as a pin—and the protective plastic over the lampshades and living-room cushions ensured it would remain so through the afterlife. The shaped soaps in the guest bathroom were also wrapped in plastic. The extra roll of toilet paper was disguised by a yellow knit hat adorned with plastic roses. Pictures of Jesus looking pained but patient hung in every room of the house except the bathroom.

There were pictures of John in every room too—outnumbering those of Jinx by about three to one.

He had been an angelic-looking altar boy, complete with cowlick and missing front tooth, and frame by frame he had grown into that dashing guy in a tux, posing with his mother on his wedding day. In between, there was a long and, probably for Nola, nerve-racking stretch of pictures of John in military garb.

I didn't think it was my imagination that John's face grew harder and grimmer in the succession of photos. War did that to people, and he seemed to have been through a lot of wars.

I was studying the family gallery when John came up behind me and rested his hands on my shoulders. I craned my neck, smiling. "I recognize Trace," I said.

John glanced at the image of himself and Trace sitting on a tank, holding beer cans and machine guns.

"Yeah, I've known Trace since high school."

I couldn't help noticing that though they both grew more wearied and weathered-looking, Trace's eyes never quite took on the bleakness in John's.

"John and Trace enlisted together," Nola said from the doorway to the kitchen.

"Like me and Andi."

John snorted, giving me a little shake, then bent his head and kissed me.

I happened to glance at Nola, and seeing her pained expression, wished I hadn't.

She chirped, "Would either of you boys like sherry?"

"God no," John said. "Why do you think I brought a bottle of wine?"

She made a *tsk-tsking* sound. "That's for dinner. We don't want to waste it."

"It's not a waste to have what you enjoy, Mamie."

She ignored that, clapping her hands together in excitement. "*Oh!* Oh, I have to show you! I've had wonderful news from the National Genealogical Society."

She bustled away, and we followed her into the living room, where she unrolled what appeared to be a large decorative descent chart.

"What do you think of that?" She beamed at John. "Of course, this is only your father's side of the family."

"I see that."

"This is the interesting part. *See?*" She pointed.

"What am I looking at?" John asked.

"Sir William Galbraith."

"What about him?"

Nola was preening over the tiny blip of Sir William Galbraith. "Well, he's a nobleman. That's the first thing. We're related to royalty! But then I did some digging. In the late spring of 1569, Sir William Galbraith conducted a justice ayre—that seems to be some kind of traveling criminal court—in Stirlingshire, where he identified and brought to trial large numbers of witches."

A witch hunter.

I stared at John.

John muttered, "Jesus."

"Yes! That's right. He was a God-fearing man. Ten of those witches were executed. Sir William continued his work until his assassination in January 1571." Nola's mouth turned down at Sir William's sad fate.

John took the chart from her, frowning as he studied it.

"A real live historical witch hunter!" Nola's eyes shined. "This is so much better than Bonnie Prince Charlie. *Everyone* claims to be related to Bonnie Prince Charlie."

I repeated faintly, "A-a *witch hunter?*"

Nola, still gloating over her genealogy chart like a pirate gazing at a treasure map, spared me a quick look. "Yes! It's right there. The ten who confessed were strangled and then burned."

A witch hunter.

John glanced at me, and his mouth curled. He said wryly, "It's all right, sweetheart; there are actually no such things as witches."

"Right."

Maybe here was the explanation for John's strange imperviousness to magic. Among the many terrifying stories regarding witch hunters was the legend that with each generation they had been less and less susceptible to spellcraft.

Which, as evolution went, made sense.

Nola, still scrutinizing the hanging tree that symbolized John's bloodline, said grimly, "If there were, it's nice to know *we* were on the right side of the law. Anyway, they all confessed."

I swallowed. "They would have been tortured first. That's how those confessions were usually obtained."

And your point is? That was Nola's expression.

John's gaze moved from her to me. He rolled up the chart and handed it to his mother. "Interesting. Are you planning to frame it?"

"Yes! Of course!"

He said to me, "Let's have a glass of wine. Dinner must be about ready?"

Nola's eyes widened. "The roast!" She laid the chart on the dining-room table and hurried into the kitchen.

I was silent as John opened the bottle of wine.

After all, it was ancient history. Every family had a few skeletons in the closet. John was no more responsible for Sir Williams's actions than I was responsible for the atrocities of Isabeau II, Countess of Abracadantès and Vosges. Granted, Isabeau had been retaliating against mortal assaults on her land and people. That was her story, anyway.

John poured the wine and handed me a glass. I tried to smile, but the smell of the dinner Nola was clucking and exclaiming over made me feel slightly sick.

John touched his glass to mine. He said very softly, "Abracadabra." He was smiling—not with understanding because I don't think he understood, but he knew I was bothered; he cared, and he was trying to let me know that he cared. That doesn't sound like much, I realize, but coming from John, it did make me feel better.

"Sit down, you two. Everything's ready," Nola called.

We took our places at the table, and Nola wafted out of the kitchen, bearing a white oval platter. "Pot roast. Just the way John likes it." She deposited the roast in the center of the table.

Apparently, the way John "liked it" was burnt to a crisp and carried to its funeral pyre on a bed of candied carrots and yams. Talk about burnt offerings.

John said, "You didn't need to go to any special effort, Mamie," clearly missing the point of all this.

"Oh, it's no effort!" She darted away again and returned with a salad bowl, which she placed next to the charred remains in the center of the linen-covered table.

"It smells delicious," I lied bravely as Nola took her place across from me.

John, at the head of the table, gave me a sardonic look and picked up the carving knife and fork. He began to hack the blackened roast apart with experience if not ease.

"Does your mother cook, Cosmo?" Nola answered her own question, "No, I suppose not, given her wealth and position. She must have a fleet of servants." Her laugh had a brittle quality to it. "I must say, it's *very* odd having a duchess in the family!"

John growled. Well, no, he cleared his throat, but it had the same effect. On me, anyway. Nola continued to blink at me with that too bright smile.

I said, "Not often. Not these days. But Maman used to make a mean omelet." That was true, but the main thing I remembered my mother making for me were delicious paper-thin crepes filled with chocolate cream. Whenever things had gone really bad at school, that had been her remedy.

There are all different kinds of magic in this world, after all.

John served the meat while Nola interrogated me for a few minutes about Maman. I think she was both impressed and offended by my mother's title. How many servants did my mother employ? How many homes did she own? Did she know any kings or queens? What did she think of American department stores? Was I actually an American citizen?

"I was born in Salem," I reminded her.

"That's true. Your father teaches there, doesn't he?"

"Yes. He teaches astronomy at Salem State University."

"But you went to college in France."

"I did, but I've lived almost my entire life in the States."

On it went. I figured this was a one-time interrogation. Nola had not really had much opportunity to grill me before John and I married.

"How is Bridget settling in?" she asked finally.

John directed a look of inquiry my way.

"Fine."

Nola beamed. "I knew she would be perfect for you. A true godsend."

I smiled politely.

The meal felt never-ending, but it did at last come to a close—whereupon we moved to the living room and Nola broke out the sherry. For another hour she regaled us with her many church activities, the witty things Father had said at mass the previous Sunday, and the silly-in-her-view exploits of her friends, who were ridiculous enough to try dating *at their age*.

John listened, commenting just often enough to prove he really was paying attention, and honestly, I loved him for that. I mean, I loved him for many reasons, but I loved that though *I* knew he was bored to tears, he was too fond of her to ever let it show.

Eventually Nola ran out of her usual conversation and turned to the thing most on her mind—besides the fond dream of reporting me to Homeland Security and having me shipped back to France. "Have you spoken to your sister since you got back?"

"No," John said. "Cosmo had lunch with her today."

"Did you?" Nola did not look particularly happy to hear this. "What did she have to say for herself?"

"I'm not sure I understand?" I threw John a questioning look. "She's working at Land of the Sun now. She seems to like it."

Nola said, "She's ignoring my phone calls."

I devoted my full attention to my sherry.

John said, "Do you think 'ignoring' might be putting it a little strongly? Maybe she's busy."

"No, I don't," Nola snapped, and even John looked a little taken aback. "And busy or not, it's disrespectful to *ignore* me. I'm her mother, and I've phoned her every single evening for the past week. She has yet to respond."

John said patiently, "I see. Did this barrage of phone calls follow an argument?"

"Of course we argued! It's impossible *not* to argue with her. She's stubborn and willful and…and…" Her gaze lit on me. "Irreverent."

I cleared my throat. John's amber gaze met mine. To my astonishment, his right eyelid lowered in the briefest of winks.

Nola came at last to what was really on her mind. "John, you're going to have to insist that Joan move back home."

I choked on my sherry.

John looked at his mother and frowned.

I cleared my throat, said—I couldn't help it—"Wait a minute. It's not fair to ask that of John. Besides, Joan isn't a child. We can't insist on any such thing. Trying to interfere in her life will only put her back up."

Which was maybe a little hypocritical, given that I didn't mind interfering in Jinx's life when I thought it was warranted. The difference was, Jinx's happiness mattered to me. I'm not sure Nola gave a damn about Jinx's happiness. In my opinion, Nola was the burn-you-at-the-stake-for-your-own-good breed.

My kind have experience with her kind, as indicated by the National Genealogical Society.

Nola pressed her thin lips together so that they almost disappeared. "Forgive me, Cosmo, but this is a family matter."

John's frown deepened into a scowl. Seeing his displeasure, Nola added hastily, "I mean only that this concerns *our* family…what's the word? *Nucleus.*"

Even if I had wanted to respond, I had no idea what to say in answer to that.

John did, though, and there was a warning note in his voice. "Mother, Cosmo *is* part of our nuclear family. Furthermore, he's the only family member Jinx might actually listen to—though it's doubtful she'll listen to him either."

I shot him a look of gratitude.

Nola, not so much. In fact, she bridled. "*You're* the head of this family, John. It's up to you to set parameters for your sister."

No wonder Jinx had moved out.

"Isn't she twenty-five?" I asked. "She has a job and her own apartment. What parameters could John reasonably set for her?"

I already wasn't high on Nola's Christmas list, and the look she shot me was one of someone planning to mail-order a truckload of coal. "You're an only child, Cosmo. I don't expect you to understand the bond between brother and sister."

"*That's enough.*" Though John spoke quietly, there was an edge to his voice. I was not surprised that reprimand brought a flush to Nola's cheeks and glitter to her eyes. I'd never heard him speak to her like that before.

I realized that he was thinking of Arabella. Thinking that Nola's words would be hurtful to me.

Maybe they should have been, but Arabella had crossed over when I was seven. I'm not sure when I finally understood she had died, but it was kind of moot because my memories of her were so vague.

Nola delivered another baleful glance my way, but to my surprise, she seemed to accept John's verdict. Or, more likely, resolved to continue the conversation when I wasn't around.

Anyway, all good things must come to an end. And all bad things as well. At long last we bade Nola good night and walked down the hill to the ferry at Larkspur Landing.

"Tired?" John asked as the lights of Nola's house disappeared around a corner.

"A little. Do you think your mother might eventually remarry?"

"No, I don't. So don't get your hopes up."

I laughed.

He turned his head my way, and I saw the glint of his teeth. "You're a good sport, Cos. Thank you for tonight."

I lifted a shoulder. "Families."

"Yes."

"In all honesty, I don't think my being there tonight helped."

John said, "It helped me."

My heart lightened.

It wasn't until we'd left the ferry terminal and were driving home that I finally brought up the subject that had been nagging at me all day.

"I'm a little worried about Ambrose."

John, adjusting the Range Rover's rearview mirror, said absently, "Why? What's wrong with Ambrose?"

"A friend of his was murdered. A woman named Abigail Starshine."

After a moment, John repeated, "Abigail Starshine?"

"Yes. In fact, I saw it on the news this morning. She was Wiccan."

It was dark in the car, but I didn't need to see John's expression to know he knew exactly who Abigail Starshine was and that he was paying close attention to my every word. He said without inflection, "And Ambrose was dating her?"

"Dating her? No. What he said was, they had been close at one time, but not recently. He was very shocked to hear she'd been killed." I wasn't sure why I added, "I think he was hoping I could tell him something about the case," because I didn't think that at all. What I *did* think was that it gave me a natural opening for asking John if he had a suspect in mind.

John said, "I don't think you want to hear about this case. I don't think either of you do. It's pretty disturbing."

"I'm sure you're right. It's only…"

John said nothing.

"If I could tell Ambrose something that might make him feel better…"

"Make him feel better about his friend being murdered?"

"You know that's not what I mean."

Silence.

I tried again. "The newscaster said there were Satanic elements to the crime. What does that even mean?"

"You know what Satanic means."

"In this context? No, I don't."

John said without inflection, "Are we going to argue about this?"

I stared at his shadowy profile. "I don't think so. Why would we? I'm not sure I understand."

"Didn't we argue once before about Satanism versus whatever your belief is supposed to be? Wicca, I suppose?"

Whatever your belief is supposed to be was not the most respectful way to put it. He had never actually asked me about my beliefs—I suspected he didn't want to know—but Wicca was an obvious conclusion to jump to. Certainly, there was overlap in the rituals and symbols and tenets of both Craft and Wicca.

John spoke out of ignorance, though, and there was nothing to be gained by taking offense.

"If you care to tell me what these elements were, I can tell you whether they're Satanic or not."

He said bluntly, "The victim was nude. She was lying in the center of an upside-down yellow chalk pentagram. Her hands and feet were nailed to the floor. A pentacle was carved into her forehead. What does that sound like to you? Wiccan or Satanic?"

He intended to shock me. Intended, I suppose, to put me in my place. Intended to make sure I never again dared to trespass—although why did he consider my asking about his case trespassing?

Anyway, two out of three wasn't bad. I was shocked. I was chastened.

I was also persistent.

I said, trying to match his unemotional tone, "It sounds Satanic, yes. Was there an athame at the...the scene?"

"What's an athame? A knife? There was something our occult expert referred to as a boline lying a few inches from the victim's hand."

I wondered briefly who SFPD's "occult expert" was. Anyone I knew?

"What did the knife look like?"

"Double-edged blade and a handle made of black wood, possibly yew."

"That's more likely an athame. A boline will usually have a single-edged blade, much sharper than that of an athame, which is supposed to be for ceremonial use only. The handle of a boline will be light, usually horn or bone or wood. I'd have to see it to be sure, but it sounds like an athame to me."

He turned his head my way, but of course in the dark interior of the car, he couldn't read my expression any better than I could his.

All he said was, "I see."

"Do you have a suspect?"

"No."

My turn to be silent. I was thinking that the good news was Ambrose was not currently a suspect in his former friend's death. Unless—and this would be the bad news—I had just brought him to the attention of the investigators by asking a lot of nosey questions.

We turned left on Hyde Street.

John said abruptly, "She wasn't the first one."

"Not the first one?"

"Not the first murder of someone within your…community."

I didn't miss the slight hesitation over that *community*. Was it distaste? Ouch. But right now, that was the least of my concerns.

"You mean another Wiccan was murdered the same way as Starshine?"

"Yes."

"One? Or more?"

"One."

"Another woman? The same method? The same—"

He said tersely, "The same MO."

Somewhere a five-bell alarm was clanging. Sick anxiety bubbled in my belly. "Are you saying—do you think this is the work of a serial killer?"

"It's looking like a strong possibility." His shadow glanced my way. "That information is to go no further. Understand?"

"Of course I understand." I spluttered, "I wouldn't— I'm not— Obviously I don't—"

"As my husband, you're going to be privy to highly sensitive information. Information that could be damaging not only to me, but to any ongoing investigations."

"I know that. I'm not an idiot."

"I know you know that. If I thought you were an idiot, I wouldn't have married you. I'm reminding you because neither of us has much experience with the other's ability to be discreet."

I said silkily, "You don't need to worry about me, *sweetheart*. I'm *well* able to keep a secret."

The silence between us was very loud as we passed a stretch of dark apartments, lightless windows and crisscrossed fire escapes, cars parked nose to bumper beneath the canopy of ficus trees. Finally, John said, "My intention wasn't to offend you. I just think it's better to lay our expectations on the table."

I continued to seethe as we turned left on Greenwich, but then, as the mortals say, reality reared its ugly head. John was right. We didn't yet know each other well enough to predict how we would behave in all circumstances. I knew John was by nature closemouthed, but I wouldn't—obviously didn't—trust him with my deepest secrets.

Granted, they were not my secrets to share.

If they were, I'd now be telling him my worry that there was a possibility—yes, a slight one, but it *was* possible—these two crimes might be connected to Seamus's murder.

Seamus had also been found with an athame lying next to him. He had not been found in a yellow chalk pentagram, but I had seen—and destroyed—evidence that his killer might have started to draw that sacred symbol. Seamus's body had not been mutilated, but again, my arrival could have interrupted the murderer's plans.

Or maybe not.

Maybe I was worrying unnecessarily.

There was a good chance the killings *weren't* connected. The other two victims were women and Wiccans. Seamus was male and Craft. And until tonight, I had been certain Seamus had died to protect the *Grimorium Primus*. Maybe it was true.

Of course, it could still be true even if Seamus *had* been killed by the same person who had slain Starshine and the other Wiccan.

If the crimes *were* connected, my tampering with crime-scene evidence was part of why Ciara was now sitting in jail.

Worst of all, I might even be partly responsible for the deaths of Abigail Starshine and this other woman.

Chapter Five

"Still mad at me?" John asked when we pulled into our parking area in front of our townhouse. His tone was rueful.

There were only a couple of other cars in our cul-de-sac. The townhouse next to ours was still dark, still empty, still under construction. The red-gold full moon rising over the bay was so huge, it looked like another world was about to bump into ours. An omen?

I sighed. "No. I'm just touchy, I guess."

John switched off the engine and half turned to face me. "You're tired. We both are. We could have used a weekend to get our bearings before having to jump right back into real life."

Real life. Yes.

"That would have been nice."

Heaven, in fact. My idea of heaven, anyway.

I could feel John's gaze; I wished I could read his face in the gloom. "I'm sorry if it sounded like I don't trust you. I do. And I love you. Very much."

That melted my heart. How could it not?

"I love you too. And I'm sorry if I seemed to be butting into things that aren't my business."

He made a sound of wry agreement and surprised me by saying, "I get it. You were afraid you'd put a bull's-eye on young Ambrose by asking about the Starshine woman. And, yes, if it hadn't been for the Hellyer case, you would certainly have spiked my interest in the kid."

Here was another reason not to mention the possible link between Seamus and the Wiccans. Ambrose had briefly been a suspect in Seamus's murder. Not for any legitimate reason—I didn't think—but one thing I'd learned about homicide investigations: detectives—like witches—do not overlook coincidences.

"Who are the detectives investigating the Starshine murder?"

"At the moment, Detectives Vincente and Chang are working the case."

"Not Iff and Kolchak?"

John's, "No," was faintly amused. "But if this case turns out to be what Chief Morrisey thinks it is, more resources will be allocated."

"Right. Of course."

He seemed to be waiting for something. When it didn't happen, he said, "Shall we go inside?"

I nodded.

I still can't get over how much you managed to get done this afternoon," John said, locking the front door behind us.

"It was mostly Bridget." No lie there. I picked up Pyewacket, gave him a quick cuddle. "You smell like catnip."

Pye's purr was self-satisfied.

"Next best thing to vodka, I suppose."

John headed toward the den. "Speaking of. Did you want a drink?"

"Sure."

A moment later Sinatra came over the stereo. "Blue Moon."

Pyewacket sprang from my arms and bounded upstairs. I followed John into the den and took a seat at the wet bar.

He poured two glasses of wine. "This is an Australian Petit Verdot."

"Ah." Wine is all right. I prefer cocktails.

His mouth twitched. He handed me a glass. "*Arriba.*"

"*Abajo.*"

"*Al centro.*" He suggestively rubbed the bowl of his glass against mine.

I grinned. "*Adentro.*"

"Abracadabra?" John asked, and my heart warmed, remembering earlier. This was how traditions were made. One morning, one evening, one glass at a time. I laughed.

"Abracadabra."

For a few peaceful minutes we sipped our wine and listened to Sinatra.

Blue moon!

Now I'm no longer alone...

Funny how your life could change so much in the space of a month. It had never occurred to me that I was lonely before I'd met John.

"What *is* a blue moon?" John mused. "Besides an optical illusion."

"The second full moon in a calendar month."

"Something rare, in other words? And that's why you named your shop Blue Moon Antiques?"

"Exactly."

For witches, that second moon, the blue moon, was an especially auspicious time for spellcasting. Lunar power reached its greatest height during a blue moon. But that wasn't something John needed to know.

I said, "I don't think you should try to order Jinx to move back home."

"I have no intention of doing so." He added, "Although I can't say I'm happy about the friends she's choosing to surround herself with."

And he probably didn't know the half of it.

"Have you met many of them?"

"No."

An uneasy thought occurred. "Are you keeping tabs on her?"

"She's not under surveillance, if that's what you mean." His smile was sardonic. "But she's my kid sister, and she's not as worldly as she thinks she is, so sure, I'm keeping an eye on her."

I sipped my wine. "Have she and your mother always been…"

"Always." He picked his glass up, contemplating the purple-red liquid. "*Is* Bridget working out?"

"So far, so good."

"Because you don't have to keep her on simply to make my mother happy."

I chuckled. "No worries. I know nothing I do will make your mother happy about me."

He grimaced. "Give her time. This is all new to her."

"It's new to us too."

"True."

"Did she not know you were gay before you told her we were engaged?"

"I can't say I ever discussed it with her. But I also never hid it."

He wouldn't have been around enough to have to hide it.

As though reading my mind, John said, "I don't think she'd have ever considered it relevant because I never showed any indication of wanting to get married."

"But then you had to go and pick, of all things, someone French."

John made a sound of amusement. "Yes. Of all things."

I finished my wine and said, "Would you mind if I walked down to the white garden for a few minutes? I'd like to see how it's coming along."

"Wouldn't you be able to see better in the daylight?"

"Well, yes, but the point of a white garden is it comes alive at night."

"Fair enough. Would you like company?"

I smiled. "Of course."

The last time I'd claimed to be in the white garden, he'd caught me lying, and I wondered if John suspected I might be lying now. He did not have a trustful nature. But I preferred to think he just wanted to keep me company.

The night air was cool and damp as we strolled down the flagstone path. Before we reached the last step, I could smell the jasmine and angel's trumpet. My heart lightened.

We reached the bottom. The garden had a hushed, magical quality to it as we stood for a moment, surrounded by glimmering, ghostly shapes. Silvery-white flagstones ringed a wide border of ivory and white heirloom roses, cream and blush-edged peonies, and panicle hydrangeas. The beds brimmed with sweet-smelling lily of the valley, snowdrops, Queen Anne's lace, fragrant white hyacinth, and choisya. Datura and angel's trumpet vines twined together as they wound around obelisks made from ornate reclaimed wrought iron. The silver and blue faux gazing ball that Ciara had blasted had been replaced with a new one, and the orbs shined like twin moons atop weathered pedestals—a reminder that John did not forget even the smallest of details.

"This is coming along," he said.

I murmured agreement, lowering myself to the marble bench. After a moment, John sat beside me. I could feel his curious gaze, but he didn't say anything else, and I was grateful for his understanding.

I was sort of ashamed of the way I'd neglected my prayers for the past two weeks. It's so important to worship when things are good and right, not just when you're in trouble.

I thought of Nola's "irreverent." She had been speaking of Jinx, but the word had come to her while looking at me.

For once, Not Guilty.

I closed my eyes and gave thanks to the Goddess. So *many* things to be thankful for now...

John took my hand as we walked back up the flagstone path.

"Were you praying?" he asked curiously.

"Yes."

He made a faint sound. Not humor exactly. Maybe a little puzzled? He said slowly, "You're such an odd mix, Cos. So blasé, even flippant about some things, and yet so...traditional in others."

I shrugged. He was right, but wasn't that true of most people? "Don't you pray?"

"No." John's voice was flat.

"But..." I tried to read his profile. "You were an altar boy for three years. You wanted a priest to marry us."

John said with unexpected harshness, "The priest was for my mother's sake. I don't believe in God, and I sure as hell don't believe in the power of prayer."

"I'm sorry."

"Don't be sorry. I'm not missing anything I can't do without, I promise you."

I had no answer, but I was troubled.

"**H**ow did I get so lucky?" John asked huskily. His big warm hand stroked me, chest to belly like he'd stroke a cat, like he'd pet his own Familiar. It felt extraordinarily nice, and if I'd known how to purr, I would have.

I laughed softly. "Do you believe in magic?"

He said, "I believe in love."

Ah, and those were indeed magic words. My cock filled, twitching like a wand at the first syllables of enchantment. I dug my heels in the mattress, arching up in invitation. Instead, his hand slid upward, stroking my chest, scratching my nipples with his thumbnail. I groaned.

"Patience is a virtue," he teased.

"I'm not feeling very virtuous."

"You don't look very virtuous, that's for sure." I could hear the smile, but also the warmth and appreciation. "You're beautiful, though. Very beautiful."

"So are you."

He made a dismissive sound, his mouth touching mine, stopping my words. He did not care for compliments. Did not trust them? I let his lips coax me into silence, opening to him in another way.

John's mouth pressing mine always made me feel that kisses were something new, something special, a secret suddenly revealed, like learning to read a map or speak a foreign language, like seeing your first blue moon rise in a night full of stars.

His was a mouth that could say some hard, even cruel things, but his kisses were so sweet, almost adoring.

His hands gathered me close, hard and competent but cherishing too. I could feel every beat of our hearts echoing in my veins and nerves, beat and answering beat. I felt safe and complete in John's arms.

His mouth lifted from mine. "What would you like?" His soft words gusted moist and warm against my ear.

I said slowly, afraid he might object to this change of dynamic, "I want to be inside you."

And he nodded, surprising me with a smile that was almost rueful. "Would you?"

"Would *you*?"

"Of course. Why not?"

He was so accepting, I was a little embarrassed to admit what I had been thinking. That a personality as dominant as John's would not consent to, let alone enjoy, taking a more... complaisant role.

"Not everyone does."

"You do."

Oh yes. I did. I loved it.

He said, "Sex is sex. What matters is giving each other pleasure." He stroked my hair back from my face. "Don't ever be afraid to tell me what you want."

"I won't." In that moment, it felt true.

We angled around, relaxed and easy, already used to each other, comfortable with each other. John stretched out before me, long and strong. Everything in beautiful proportion, the ripple of muscles beneath supple skin, the red-gold dusting of hair over limbs and genitals. His hands and feet were carefully groomed, the nails trimmed and buffed. His hair was neatly cut, the rebel wave controlled. The expensive suits, love of fine wine, appreciation for antiques—he presented a cultured image to the world, but beneath the veneer was something not so civilized, not so careful. Now and then it flickered through his hawk-colored eyes. A familiarity with violence, with cruelty.

But familiarity was not pleasure. I wrapped my arms around his broad shoulders, wanting, illogically, to shelter him from all the painful things he had faced. I kissed the back of his strong neck, and he shivered.

"I love you," I whispered. "I never knew it was possible to love anyone like this."

He made a soft sound, not laughing at me, maybe not quite believing me.

The small bottle of Happy Endings sat on the nightstand next to the bed, and I drizzled the slick and pleasantly scented oil over my fingers. I separated the taut globes of John's buttocks with one hand and probed that puckered little opening with the other.

I delicately pushed one finger in, and John uttered a long, low groan, his body clenching.

"Is it all right?" I leaned forward, pressed a damp kiss between his shoulder blades. The ring of muscle pulled at my finger as I slid in and out. "Do you like it?"

I did. I liked everything we did.

"Is…that…a…serious…question?" he gulped.

I took my time, not so much because John needed it, but because I did. I felt weak and trembly at the idea of what was ahead, afraid he wouldn't like it, that I might do it wrong, might disappoint him, or worst of all, accidentally harm him…shaken that he trusted me, loved me enough to let me do this. Although I could tell he didn't really need it, I pressed a second finger in, stretching him, seeking that nub of nerves and gland. John pushed back at my hand, drawing me in deeper.

"You're very skilled…" He turned his head, smiling.

"Are you surprised?"

"Not at all. The surprise was…" He didn't finish it, but I knew what had surprised him. "I knew the first time you wrapped that pretty mouth around my dick…*oh fuuuck…*" His whole body arched as I found his prostate.

I moved forward, trying to find his mouth at that awkward angle, kissing instead the point of his jaw, the damp hollow behind his ear, all the while still lightly, deliberately massaging the spongy bump. My own cock was rock hard, my balls aching. My heart slammed with desperate longing. John shuddered as I lowered myself on top of him. The hard heat of his body down the length of mine was the sweetest torture.

"Say something in French," he gasped.

"Huh?" I gave an unsteady laugh. "Like what?"

"Anything," he groaned. "I just like to hear you. You could order pancakes and I'd think it was sexy."

Laughter, love, swelled in my chest. I muttered shakily, "*Puis-je avoir du sirop avec mes pancakes?*"

John laughed breathlessly. "Go on…"

I dropped my head to his back. I could feel the hard thump of his heart against my hot face. "*Non.* You make me shy."

I think it surprised both of us. He slid free, turned, taking me in his arms. I tried to bury my face in his shoulder, but he raised my chin with his finger. "No way, *ma belle.* You're not the shy type." He was amused, but gentle too.

I made a little face at the feminine *ma belle*. Said only, "With you, I am. I don't know why."

"Don't be. You don't ever have to…" He didn't finish it, but it was okay. Even that much was more than he usually gave.

I said softly, "*C'est tellement bon.* I didn't think anything could feel better than the other way, *mais c'est exquis.*"

"Yeah?" His hand insinuated itself between the hot press of our bodies, closed around my cock.

Words failed me. I moaned softly, desperately, pushing into his grip.

"I have something nicer for you," he said.

He did too.

We changed position again, and John's buttocks humped back against my groin as my cock took the place of my fingers in that moist heat. So… *good.* I whimpered as his sphincter muscle contracted around me. Began to push and slide in that hot darkness. Instinct. I couldn't have stopped to save my life.

John let out a deep sound, something between a groan and a growl, and began to rock back hard against me. I thrust back at him, closing my eyes, just concentrating on that welcome velvet grab, trying to push deeper, needing to feel joined, united. Heat on burning heat. His fierce silence in contrast to my own wounded sounds as I pumped into him, reaching further and further for that desperate release—

And finally…the sweetest of surrenders rising up out of the yearning to unite, the falling away of all barriers, all doubts and fears and questions swept aside in the dizzying tide of thrust and drop, push and pull…slow, sweet climax that pulsed through me, warming me with every heartbeat.

"John… John…" I couldn't help it. Couldn't help the helpless noises as I began to come, opening my heart's wings, pouring out silly, emotional things while my muscles turned to jelly and my cock spurted sticky release into the clench of his channel. We flew straight into the blazing stars.

I collapsed on top of him, gasping for breath, quivering head to foot. I'm embarrassed to confess I didn't even know if he'd come. I hoped so. The sheets were damp, the room scented of sex and John.

A long, long time later, John stirred, rolling over, tumbling me into his arms. He drew the covers over us, cradling me against his warmth. He kissed my brow bone and my nose, and I smiled, opened sleepy eyes.

Over his shoulder, I could see Pyewacket in the window, his eyes glowing.

Chapter Six

On Saturday the honeymoon ended.

Perhaps I exaggerate.

Probably not.

John was fixing pancakes and promising that next weekend would be different. Next weekend we would sleep late—nine or so—and then he'd fix us a "real" breakfast. I believe the gory details included creamed chipped beef and buckwheat cakes. Oh, and screwdrivers.

I don't like orange juice or breakfast, and my idea of sleeping late on a weekend is noonish. Assuming I *have* to be somewhere that afternoon.

I smiled bravely through this litany of horrors, which appeared to be the correct response, and he returned to whisking flour, salt, baking powder, sugar, Ajax detergent, and whatever else was going into my antique Wedgewood basalt basin. I mean, they have boxed mixes for this very sort of occasion.

"You're going to be here today, right?"

"Hm?" I was trying to read—without looking like I was trying to read—the article about Abigail Starshine's murder on the front page of the *Chronicle*. I was horrified to see the headline: Police Baffled by Second Witch Killer Slaying.

Witch Killer.

The press had given the murderer or murderers a nickname.

"Cos?"

I stared blankly at John.

"Are you here all day?"

"What? No. I've got to go in to the shop."

His brows drew into a straight line. "I thought we discussed this? Someone's got to be here today. The contractor is coming to see about the pool."

I stared at him. The *pool*?

John's brows rose. "I know we talked about this. About putting a pool in the backyard."

"We talked yes, but I didn't think it was decided. I don't…"

Want a pool.

It would be hard to think of anything I wanted less.

John was looking at me in inquiry.

"It's just, I'm not so sure a pool is a great idea."

"What's your objection?"

"Well, it will take up most of the top garden. The yard will be all deck and pool."

"Correct. That's good for entertaining."

"Yes, I suppose so. But."

"But what?" John asked. I could see he was growing a little impatient.

"I can't swim."

In fact, I was terrified of water—maybe because my cousin Waite had tried to drown me when we were kids.

John looked surprised. "You can't swim at all?"

"At all. I sink. Like a stone."

He smiled. "That's not a problem. I'll teach you to swim. It'll be fun."

Yeeeah. No. It really wouldn't.

"Okay, thank you. I appreciate the offer. But I don't even *like* water."

"I'm sorry to hear it," John said. "But I still would like a pool. It's good exercise—yes, I know you also hate exercise, but it would be good for you to do something physical once in a while—and it's good for property value."

I was a little offended by the good-for-you-to-do-some-thing-physical-once-in-a-while comment—especially consider-ing the night before—and I was a lot offended by the fact that we were obviously going to have a pool whether I wanted it or not.

But it wasn't fair to be angry if I wasn't going to be honest, so I said, "It isn't just... I-I have a fear of water."

That wasn't easy to admit. John wasn't someone with much tolerance for weakness of any kind, and I didn't want to admit this vulnerability.

He said briskly, "Then this will be a good way for you to overcome that fear."

He wasn't even curious about what had caused my fear. The cause was irrelevant, the fear dismissed as of no impor-tance.

But it was not a surprise.

He was already moving on. "So if you could manage to be here to meet with Fred?"

"Fred?"

"Our contractor."

Now he was *our* contractor.

I folded my lips together against the indignant things on the tip of my tongue. After all, John had given me half the backyard for my white garden, and my being afraid of water wasn't really a legitimate reason for denying him a swimming pool.

Maybe he was right. Maybe this would be the way to over-come my fear.

"What time is Fred coming by?"

"Three."

"All right. I'll make sure I'm home in time to talk to him."

John nodded approvingly and slid a couple of fluffy, golden pancakes on my plate. "Did you want jam or syrup?"

"Nutella."

He blinked. "I guess it's true. You think you know some-one…"

"Ha."

He turned to the still mostly empty cupboards. "Do we actually own a jar of Nutella?"

"Somewhere." I gave up. Sighed. "Raspberry jam is fine."

John smiled approvingly, unscrewed the raspberry jam, and handed it over. "There you go. Take notes this afternoon. We can finalize the details over dinner."

* * * * *

To my relief, Ambrose was behind the counter talking to Blanche when I arrived at Blue Moon Antiques.

Blanche gave me a look over the top of her glasses that I think was supposed to mean *Don't Be Too Hard on Him.*

"Step into my web," I invited, holding the office door.

Ambrose trudged into my office as though walking the plank. "I'm sorry about yesterday," he began.

I leaned against the desk, resting my tailbone on top. "Yesterday was understandable," I said. "I'm less happy about the week I left for my honeymoon, but even then, stuff happens. Family emergencies, transportation strikes, parole-board hearings…"

He looked alarmed.

I continued, "I don't care about your missing a day of work here and there. What's worrying me is I don't think you're telling me the truth." I corrected, "That is, I think you're telling me part of the truth, but there's a lot you're not telling me."

He opened his mouth, but I headed him off. "The part you're not telling me scares you. And *that's* what worries me."

He changed color, said defensively, "If you don't want me to work for you—"

"What? That's not what I'm saying. Not at all."

He stared down at his worn Nikes, his expression closed.

"Ambrose."

He raised his long lashes, flicked me a dark, unreadable look, went back to staring at his tennis shoes.

I sighed. "I wish you could trust me a little."

He said slowly, "Mr. Grindlewood told me you might want to interfere in things that…"

"In things that what?"

He met my gaze. "Aren't your business."

I couldn't think of anything to say. My confusion must have shown because Ambrose shrugged and returned to not looking at me.

He murmured, "That's what he said."

There were so many responses, I didn't quite know where to begin. First off, the kid wasn't just my employee, he was my apprentice, which meant everything he did—everything he *thought*—was my fucking business. Secondly, even if he had been just my employee, *someone* needed to take an interest in his life, and Ralph had pretty much landed Ambrose on me. Granted, Ralph had changed his mind and tried to get me to throw Ambrose back in—and what was that about? I still couldn't make sense of it. Thirdly and finally…

"When did Mr. Grindlewood say that?" I asked mildly.

"Last night."

That was a shock. I had assumed—and now I wondered why—that Ambrose would not continue to socialize, if that was the word for it, with Ralph after Ralph had tried to poison the well against him. But Ambrose had no idea Ralph was the one who had brought Ambrose's juvenile criminal record to my attention.

"Ah," I said.

Ambrose watched me warily, which led me to believe Ralph had probably said something to the effect that I might try to discourage their friendship—and that was absolutely the truth. If I hadn't been forewarned, I'd have done exactly that.

I said, "That seems a little unfair of Mr. Grindlewood, but it's certainly true that the relationship between apprentice and master is a close one. Or should be." I spread my hands. "Very well. I'll do my best not to trespass. Have you started your grimoire?"

Ambrose looked confused, whether at my abrupt change of subject or the fact that I was already asking for his homework. "Not yet, no. There hasn't been time."

I shook my head. Not that I was surprised, but I was a little disappointed.

He said quickly, "I'll try to start tonight."

"Good." I pointed at the door. "I'm sure Blanche has a mile-long list for you."

Ambrose rose, hesitated, then went out.

I tried again to reach my mother.

And again, Phelon was not particularly helpful. "If she doesn't want to talk to me, I can't see why she'd want to talk to you."

"I can."

"Well, I can't." He added spitefully, "Aren't you supposed to be on your honeymoon or something? Bored with your mortal already?"

From this I deduced that Maman and her companion were quarreling. Not for the first time. But even that couldn't cheer me up.

Nor was my mood improved when I phoned Our Lady of the Green Veil hospital and learned Rex was still in a coma. Nor, because I was not family, would anyone venture a prognosis.

"Bad news?" Blanche asked when she brought me the mail a little while later.

"I don't know. Do you think it's true that no news is good news?"

She made a face. "Not necessarily."

"Same."

I idly spun the letter opener on its point. We watched silently as it twirled, glinting each time sunlight struck the blade.

I said to her, "Have you ever come across a woman named Valenti Garibaldi?"

Blanche looked wry. "Mr. Grindlewood's new girlfriend?"

"That's the one."

She said dryly, "The self-professed Witch Queen. Yes. I've heard of her."

"What's her story?"

"Good question. I know she claims seven Bay Area covens as her hives."

"Claims? That's verifiable, right?"

"You would think. I've been part of the Wiccan community for longer than you've been alive, and I never heard of her until last year."

I thought that over. In the mortal realm, a Witch Queen is mostly an honorary title bestowed on one who has achieved the position of High Priestess of the Third Degree or higher and who has gone on to teach and groom several *other* High Priestesses or High Priests who have *also* reached Third Degree or higher and subsequently founded a *minimum* of five covens propagating the beliefs and rituals of the Witch Queen's chosen tradition.

I mean, it varied, depending on traditions, but not significantly. Bottom line: you can't claim the title for yourself, and it takes a hella long time to reach that exalted status. In my experience, at least twenty years. If Valenti was a genuine Witch Queen, she'd started her training when she was ten.

Granted, I'd started my training when I turned five. Not because I would one day be *L'ermite*, but because that's how it works in the Craft.

But of course, I couldn't tell Blanche that.

I said, "She could be from out of town."

"She could be from off-world, for all I know," Blanche said. "But if she's a transplant, how is it she has seven local hive-covens?"

Good question.

Valenti was definitely a witch. She might be Wiccan as well, though I'd never known that to happen before. Still. Did that mean her covens were Craft? If so, I was more anxious about Jinx than ever.

On the other hand, did these covens even exist?

"Do you know anyone who belongs to one of her covens?" I asked.

Blanche shook her head, but then said, "The girl who was murdered the other night. Abigail Starshine. She was supposed to be one of Garibaldi's High Priestesses."

"*A High Priestess?* That wasn't in the news. I didn't hear that anywhere."

"Newly anointed. I don't think it was widely known."

Or known at all outside of sacred circles.

I said, "Did you know the other woman who was killed? Somebody Hellyer?"

"No."

"Do you know anything about her?"

Blanche shook her head. "I could ask around if you like."

"Yes, but be discreet." She nodded, and I said, "And by discreet, I mean be *very* careful. The only thing any of us know for sure is it's open season on witches."

* * * * *

I've never visited anyone in jail before. I was arrested once, but my jailhouse experience was not most people's jailhouse experience—not that most people *have* jailhouse experience.

Anyway, the Craft has a long and unhappy history with incarceration, and I can't pretend that even walking into that huge complex on 7th Street—which actually houses two separate jails—didn't fill me with extreme anxiety.

Per the online instructions, I arrived in the lobby ten minutes before my appointment to fill out additional paperwork. I was patted down for the second time, my ID was checked—beyond some stone-faced guard verifying that I matched my photo, no one seemed to pay undue attention—and I was at last escorted to a small room where Ciara sat at a small table. A uniformed guard stood near a vending machine that looked like it had been there since the 1960s.

"I wasn't sure you would come," Ciara said.

"Neither was I," I admitted, taking the chair across from her. I glanced uneasily at the security cam pointed our way.

"Thank you."

I shrugged. "Is there something I can do for you?"

She had lost weight over the past two weeks—and she had not been a large woman to start with. Her green eyes looked muddy in her gaunt face. Her skin was dull, her strawberry-blonde hair lank. She looked like anyone would look after two weeks of jail.

Ciara said, "You can buy me a Pepsi and listen to what I have to say."

I bought her the Pepsi—the guard had to kick the machine to get it to work—and sat down at the table again.

"I didn't kill Seamus," she said.

"Presumably that's why you've hired Sjoberg. To prove it in a court of law."

She nodded, gazing down at her knotted hands. "They're saying I killed him out of jealousy. That he was having an affair with another woman."

"Someone named V.," I said. "Do you know who that would be?"

"No. There was no affair."

I hesitated. Seamus had always been, well, a player. Maybe he had changed after his marriage, but maybe he hadn't. Wasn't the wife supposedly always the last to know? Finally, I said, "You know they found letters on his computer, right?"

"Yes." Her face twisted. "I don't care what they found. I don't deny that he might have flirted, fooled around. It wouldn't have been serious for Seamus."

"How can you be so sure?"

"It wasn't the first time. It wouldn't have been the last time. It's just the way he was. He flirted as easily as he breathed. It never went far. He never broke his vow to me. He remained my beloved consort."

That could be the truth, but I understood why the cops were not impressed. Jealousy is part of the human condition. Ciara's apparent confidence was not only unusual, it was probably downright annoying. I believed her, though. Not so much about her stated lack of jealousy as her insistence she hadn't killed Seamus. For reasons previously noted.

I said, "Let's say I do believe you. I'm not sure what you think I can do about this. From a legal standpoint—"

She said impatiently, "I'm not asking for *legal* help from you. I'm asking you to go to the Duchess. If you tell her you believe me when I say I didn't kill Seamus, if you ask her to intercede on my behalf—"

"But you're not Abracadantès. You're *buidseachd*."

"The Abracadantès is ten times more powerful than the *buidseachd*."

"Well, yes. Even so."

Her chin lifted. For a moment her eyes blazed with the old passion. "I'm the lawful consort of a witch of the Abracadantès tradition. I'm entitled to claim protection from the Society. I know you and Seamus weren't friends, but you *owe* him for sending you the—"

"Be silent," I warned her.

The guard studied us thoughtfully.

Ciara pressed her lips together. Her eyes remained defiant.

I considered her sternly. Would she have blurted out the name of the *Grimorium Primus* if I hadn't stopped her? I believed so. She was just as reckless and headstrong as Seamus.

"How do you know about that?"

Her smile was bitter. "News travels. Even behind these walls."

Yes. That I believed. News travels everywhere.

As though reading my mind, Ciara said, "I'm formally asking you as the Duc of Westlands to petition your mother to go to the Société du Sortilège on my behalf and invoke their help. Otherwise, it's pretty clear I'm going to spend the rest of my life in prison."

I flinched as she added the name of the Society and my title to the other sacred names she'd revealed. This room was almost certainly bugged, and everything we said was likely being recorded. But maybe in her position, I'd be that desperate too. Everything Ciara had said was true. I did owe Seamus for sending me the grimoire—for saving the grimoire—and she did have a right to the help and protections of the Abracadantès.

And more to the point, she was innocent.

I knew perfectly well she had not killed Seamus. She *had* tried to kill me, and more than once, but if someone killed John? I couldn't guarantee I wouldn't try to repay the favor. Tenfold.

"Assuming you *are* innocent, who do you think killed Seamus—and why?"

"This woman V. Whoever she is. It must be her."

I didn't expect that. I thought she would make the connection I had. That Seamus's death was directly tied to his recovery of the great grimoire. "But why would she kill him?"

"*Triùir a thig gun iarraidh: gaol, eud is eagal.*"

"I don't know what that means."

"Three that come unbidden: love, jealousy, and fear."

"I still don't follow."

"When she realized Seamus was simply having a little fun at her expense, she took her revenge."

A woman scorned? Maybe. It seemed unlikely to me, but I was no expert on women.

"All right," I said. "I'll speak to the Duchess. I don't think I'll have to convince her to go to the Society. Seamus did save the GP, and we all owe him a debt of gratitude for that."

Her face twisted. "Yes, you do. It doesn't bring him back, though."

Chapter Seven

I should make something clear.

As great as my familiarity is with mortal television and cinema, particularly when it comes to anything to do with the occult or witchcraft, one thing I've never had any interest in is crime or mystery shows. Yes, I am familiar, of course, with the adventures of the great witch Jessica Fletcher—her character is clearly coded as, at the very least, Wiccan—but I personally never had the slightest interest in who killed Professor Plum in the Conservatory. Let alone why.

Which means that my uneasy knowledge that I needed to understand whether there was a connection between Seamus's murder and the murder of two Wiccans, left me unhappily aware of how totally unqualified I was for the task.

I had zero idea how to set about sleuthing—and no resources for such an endeavor.

Jessica Fletcher would have started asking questions of all her neighbors and friends, but I didn't have to try it to know my neighbors and friends would not be nearly as forthcoming as the mortals of Cabot Cove.

My attempt to get information from John hadn't gone well, and I knew that avenue was closed. In fact, I would have to be very, very careful John didn't find out I was tentatively pursuing…whatever it was I was pursuing.

I wasn't sure.

When I got back from meeting with Ciara, I tried searching on the Internet for information on Abigail Starshine. There was a lot more information on her death than there was on her life.

Worse, my haphazard searching brought up a whole host of "Wiccan" murders. And by that, I mean crimes mischaracterized by the police or the press as witch or Wiccan related. There was the elderly mother and two sons murdered in Florida and dubbed by the media the "Blue Moon" murders. There was the witch in New Mexico who stabbed to death a man during some travesty of a Beltane sex ritual. Not counting the Starshine homicide, those were the most recent crimes, but there were a bunch of others, equally gruesome and with equally tenuous ties to witchcraft and Wicca. It was depressing as hell—and I do literally mean Hell.

In Abigail Starshine's case, she arrived home on Thursday night, had a glass of wine to unwind, went to bed, and was attacked sometime during the night. I skimmed the horrific details of the crime itself, trying to understand what conclusions, if any, the police were sharing with the press.

One alarming aspect of the murder was that it seemed the attacker had already been in the house when Abigail arrived home; another was that, apparently, the wine she drank was laced with sleeping pills. Police speculated that the wine had been a gift, though there was no information as to why they thought so.

As far as I could tell, the modus operandi of Abigail's murder had nothing in common with Seamus's. Well, they had both been stabbed, possibly with their own ceremonial daggers, but that was about it. And that was a relief. In addition to the obvious differences, Seamus had been attacked in his shop. He had most likely admitted his killer.

It wasn't proof that the cases were unrelated. Troubling similarities remained, but these occult elements were broad and general: athames beside the bodies, and the possibility that, had I not interrupted the killer, a pentagram would have encircled Seamus's body as well.

One unknown element was whether the same sigil I had seen that night at the Creaky Attic—the projection of an old-time witch on her broomstick—had been present at the other crime scenes. The magic-lantern projection was not something that would have still been visible once the crime-scene technicians arrived.

The problem—one problem—was that I did not think like a police officer. I did not even think like a police commissioner.

I remembered when I'd asked John about the investigation into Seamus's death, he told me the investigation begins with the victim. Detectives would examine every aspect of these women's lives. They would check their finances and their employment history. They would talk to friends, enemies, family, lovers, neighbors. They would certainly examine their religious life—and I shuddered to think what clumsy conclusions they would draw.

John had also said there were no secrets in a murder investigation, but that was the goal, not the reality.

I had no way of conducting that kind of investigation. And even if I had, I wouldn't have known what I was looking for.

I tried searching for a recent murder victim by the name of Hellyer and immediately got dozens of hits. I read the results with fascinated horror.

Clara Hellyer had been killed while John and I were in Scotland. These crimes were happening in quick succession.

Like Abigail, she had drunk drugged wine before being stabbed to death. Her body was nude and nailed to the floor, positioned within the five points of a pentagram. She was found with a pentacle carved in her forehead.

Unlike Abigail, police believed—at least originally—that Clara had invited her killer to enter her home.

Someone she knew, then?

That made sense. If the drugged wine had been gifted to Abigail by someone she knew—thought she knew—it made more sense. Snow White wasn't eating random fruit. She thought she knew the old crone with the basket of apples. She imagined a friendship where there was none.

Interestingly, although the occult elements of the crime were obvious, neither the press nor the police had initially made the connection to Clara's religious affiliation. It looked to me like no one had connected the dots until Abigail had been killed.

It was after Abigail that the media began speculating a serial killer was stalking San Francisco's Wiccan community. The police were still neither confirming nor denying. It was the media that had given the killer the nickname Witch Killer.

All of which left me where?

"I didn't know you could cook," John said over dinner that evening. He took another forkful of paella à la Granada. "Not like this."

"But I'm doing the food on Sunday."

"I figured you'd end up hiring caterers."

"Ye of little faith!"

He acknowledged it. Said appeasingly, "This is delicious."

I sniffed. "Thank you." I rose to top up his glass with white Rioja.

Not to preen, but yes, I am a very good cook. It's my one claim to domestic fame. Unless mixologist counts. Which it probably doesn't. I won't deny that a pinch of Craft, a dash of magic, can help things along, but I actually find cooking so relaxing, I rarely resort to spellcraft.

In addition to paella, tonight's meal included gazpacho, green salad, and toasted French bread.

John held his glass up to me. "Candlelight, a great meal, the right wine. If I'd realized marriage could be like this, I wouldn't have waited so long."

"I *think* that's a compliment. Not sure."

John drained half his glass, grinned, started to respond, but the phone rang. He grimaced. "You sit down and eat. I've got it." He pushed his chair back and stepped into the hall.

A moment later I heard his slightly weary, "Hi, Pete."

A feeling of unease slid down my spine. It was nearly seven. Wasn't that late for a phone call from Sergeant Bergamasco? Then again, John had warned me early on that Police Commissioner was not a nine-to-five job.

I sipped my wine, listening to the prolonged silence from the hallway, and my disquiet grew.

Whatever this was, it was not good news.

"I see." John's tone was flat. "Thanks for calling."

Silence.

"Yes. You too."

I heard him replace the phone. The floorboards squeaked as he returned to the dining room.

"That was Sergeant Bergamasco," he said, retaking his seat at the table.

"I heard. Is there a problem?"

The candlelight cast severe shadows across his hard cheekbones and dark eyes. He said evenly, "I think there is, yes. I understand you visited Ciara Reitherman this morning."

Oh shit.

I felt myself changing color. "I—yes. I did."

"Is there some reason you didn't want to tell me about it yourself?"

Several reasons—though I couldn't admit that—starting with the scant hope that John wouldn't find out.

"Frankly? I didn't think you'd want me to go, and I felt that I needed to hear what she had to say."

"Why?"

"I-I'm not sure I understand?"

"Why did you feel you needed to hear what she had to say?"

I didn't want to lie to him. I had promised to never lie to him. I floundered, "Because maybe it concerned me?"

He drew a sharp breath, which he then let out slowly, quietly. "Cos, does it not occur to you that by visiting this woman, you're not only jeopardizing the case against her, you're very likely reinstating yourself as a possible suspect in Reitherman's death?"

No, to be honest, neither of those things had occurred to me.

I protested, "What? That's ridiculous!"

"It's not ridiculous at all. Her defense could try to claim that a relationship exists between the two of you, that together, and for reasons not yet known to the prosecution, you concocted a scheme to get rid of Reitherman's husband, and then for reasons unknown, fell out."

"Nobody would believe that for a minute. What would my motive be?"

"Motive is irrelevant. Motive can always be found if the other pieces of the puzzle are in place."

"But the other pieces aren't in place."

John said, "Not all of them, no. But enough are. Which is why you fell under suspicion the first time around. I can't believe you blithely strolled into that interview room for a chat with the woman who tried to kill you."

"She asked to speak to me."

John pressed his lips together. He took the time to refill his wineglass. He held the bottle up. I shook my head.

He said carefully, and I could hear that greatly strained patience, "The main reason you're no longer under suspicion is because she is."

"Yes, but she shouldn't be. I told you I didn't think she murdered Seamus, and she confirmed it."

"She… Cos." For about a split second, John looked truly at a loss.

"I believe her."

"That's nice. Given that she tried to kill you. In front of about fifty witnesses, several of whom belong to SFPD. For that alone, they're going to lock her up and, hopefully, throw away the key."

I was dismayed by his casual brutality.

"She thought I killed Seamus."

"Don't repeat that," John warned.

"It's the truth."

"If it *is* the truth, it strengthens the case against you."

I saw his point.

I also saw that, being unable to share all the facts of the situation, continuing to try to convince him of anything was a waste of time.

I said quietly, "You're right. I didn't think about how things might look or how my visit might potentially affect Ciara's case. And I realize that you're concerned for me. I truly believe her when she says she didn't kill Seamus, but I can see that I should have spoken to you before I went to see her."

He relaxed a little. "I don't think any real harm has been done. You're…an unusual person, Cos. People, my people, don't always understand—are liable to misinterpret your actions."

He was not only serious, he was earnest, and I was touched to see his worry for me.

"I know. It's all right. I don't care what people think."

John said, "I have to care, though."

Once more I felt heat flood my face. "Yes. Right. I didn't mean—"

"I know you didn't kill Reitherman. I know you're genuinely worried about a perceived injustice."

"Well, yes." *Aren't you?* That was my real question. I didn't have to ask it because John continued in his blunt, dogged way.

"When the Reitherman woman came after you, she lost any sympathy I might have had for her. There's more than enough evidence to put her away forever, and that's fine with me."

"But if she didn't do it—"

"She'll have done something else. She did do something else. She tried to harm *you*."

I think he saw my shock, because something glinted in his eyes for a moment. Regret? Guilt? Shame? If so, it was gone in the blink of an eye.

I said, "I can't believe you mean that, John. I know you don't really."

Instead of answering, he said, "Promise me you'll stay away from her. I want your word that you won't do anything else to jeopardize the case against her."

"John."

"I'm deadly serious about this."

He was too. It was right there on his face.

I said, "I...I'm not... I don't know how to answer that. I'm not trying to interfere or make trouble for you. She asked for my help, and—"

"Your word." John was adamant.

I gazed into his face and understood a couple of hard truths that had escaped me before. Magical abilities notwithstanding, John really *did* hold all the power in our relationship. And although he had not included "obey" in our wedding vows, my obedience was clearly a condition of our marriage.

The ability to negotiate a hard bargain is the ability to walk away from a bad deal. John—it was right there in the fierce lines of his face, in the steely gleam of his eyes—was prepared—*always* prepared—to walk away. I was not. Could not even contemplate it. Not then.

In those four minutes I learned more about him than I'd learned in four weeks, and I'm ashamed to admit I crumbled.

I said huskily, "I promise."

The flinty look faded. We were no longer on opposite sides of the battlefield. "Thank you."

There must have been something in my face, in my eyes, because his expression grew gentle, apologetic.

He leaned forward to take my hand, his lips brushing across my knuckles and sending a little shiver of pained pleasure down my back. "Thank you, sweetheart."

He was not relenting, not in any way, but he was truly sorry for having to be harsh, for having to insist.

That night our lovemaking was especially passionate.

John was, if possible, more attentive and tender than ever before, and I could see that he recognized I was a little stiff, a little closed, and he was patient, even sympathetic in his wooing of me. Sure, he had won the battle—he planned on winning all our battles—but he was generous in victory, trying to show with every lingering, loving caress the rewards of surrender.

And I can't pretend that I didn't respond, didn't let myself be petted and comforted and reassured. I loved him.

When he whispered roughly, "There's nothing as important to me as you," I wanted to believe him.

I even did believe him a little.

But my heart was still heavy.

Chapter Eight

Everyone wants to believe their job matters. Myself included.

Which is why I made a point of attending estate sales, although both Antonia and Blanche used to tell me Blue Moon was too high-end to carry other people's cast-offs. Anyway, *all* antiques are other people's cast-offs.

When elderly people cross, especially people with no kith or kin, very often their belongings end up in yard sales, or on the shelves of charity organizations like Goodwill, or, sadly, in dumpsters. It's no different in the Craft. The difference is, an elderly witch's worldly goods are almost certain to contain items both sacred and magical. Items that could be dangerous in the wrong hands.

Long before I knew of the Society for Prevention of Magic in the Mortal Realm, I made it a point to collect such items so that they could be safely passed on to another of the Craft.

Now that I knew of SPMMR, I felt it all the more imperative that these items not fall into hostile hands. In fact, this was a subject I planned to eventually bring to the attention of the Société du Sortilège. Not that I thought much would come of it. The Craft is not good at organizing campaigns, especially across traditions.

Anyway, on Sunday morning I was attending the estate sale of Hazel Nottingham in Roseville.

Hazel had been ninety-three when she crossed. She was Craft, though not Abracadantès. We had not been friends, but we had been friendly, and over the years I'd sold her a few rather valuable antiquarian (i.e., occult) texts—books I was now eager to retrieve, if at all possible. Hazel had no children of her own, and her great-niece was both mortal and unsentimental. The niece had hired AM Schiff & Company to liquidate her aunt's estate, and by the time Blanche and I arrived, Hazel's treasures were disappearing fast.

"These are sweet," Blanche said, stopping to examine a display of modern Capodimonte porcelain.

"Focus," I said, scanning the rows of long tables stacked with books and bric-a-brac.

"On what?"

I didn't reply, astonished to see a familiar figure—small, spindly, with white hair that looked like the tousled feathers of a dalmatian pelican—speaking eagerly to another man. My heart skipped a beat as I recognized the second man.

Ralph Grindlewood.

"Blessed be," Blanche said. "Isn't that Oliver Sandhurst?"

"Yes."

"I haven't seen him in ages."

I opened my mouth, but I had no idea what to say. I'd been so sure Oliver had met with some terrible fate, and that that fate might be my fault. But here he was, looking perfectly normal—for Oliver—chatting pleasantly with Ralph as if they were old friends. *Ralph.* The enemy of everything Oliver and I devoted our lives to protecting and preserving.

Was it possible that Oliver didn't know about the Society for Prevention of Magic in the Mortal Realm? Was it possible Oliver still believed Ralph was a friend and not a foe?

Here was a worse thought: was it possible Oliver was working with SPMMR?

"Oh, and there's Mr. Grindlewood," Blanche said. "He had the same idea as us."

No lie there.

"We need to find those books," I said, turning my back on Oliver and Ralph. I didn't think they had spotted Blanche or me yet. They didn't seem to be in any hurry, continuing to shoot the breeze while potential buyers inched past or leaned around them to examine the items spread across the long tables filling Hazel's front yard.

"What books?" Blanche asked.

"I sold Hazel a 1958 first edition of *Nedoure: Priestess of the Magi or Blazing Star*, and I know she had a copy of the 1929 translation of *Compendium Maleficarum*."

"Ugh. Why would you want a copy of *that*?"

"I don't. I also don't want copies of it floating around."

Blanche looked confused, and I couldn't blame her. It's not as though I could confiscate all copies of one of the most insidious and vicious of the witch-hunter handbooks. Even if that were possible, versions of the book would continue to linger on the Internet for eternity.

Still. Physical copies have far more power than any representation. No need to make it easy for our enemies.

I said, "There are books stacked over there. Near the table with the clocks. Let's split up. You start from the left; I'll take the tables on the right. If you see anything rare or valuable of an occult nature, grab it."

Blanche, still looking a little perplexed, nodded and headed in the direction of the book tables. I went in the opposite direction, trying to avoid catching the eye of either Oliver or Ralph.

I learned two things about Hazel that day: she had a taste for historical romances with covers featuring brawny, bare-chested men in kilts, and, over the years, she had consumed a bakery's worth of Danish butter cookies. Hazel had an extensive collection of books, some sacred, some secular, some valuable, some not, but the day's prize was a battered black-leather journal. A couple of pressed flowers and herbs slipped out when I opened the book. I glanced at browned pages of ink drawings and Latin notations.

Her grimoire.

I held it against my chest for a moment.

Don't worry. It's safe now. I'll keep it safe.

"Cosmo," Ralph said from beside me, and I jumped. "I should have expected to see you here."

He was smiling, blue eyes twinkling with familiar good-humor. It was strange—knowing what I did now—but I had trouble reconciling my old concept of Ralph with my new understanding of who and what he was. He did not look remotely dangerous.

He still looked like a friend.

It was troubling.

"Ralph," I said. "How are you?"

"Very well. Very well indeed." His smile broadened. "How are you enjoying married life?"

"It's nice. I'm a fan."

"Excellent. You and John make a charming couple. How did you enjoy Scotland?"

"It's beautiful."

If my answers struck him as half-hearted, he gave no sign.

"Were you able to visit any of the ten sites of arcane power?"

Was he fucking *insane*?

To speak of these things in broad daylight?

I stared at him, truly at a loss how to answer. I had thought I knew him. I had thought he was a friend. Not just my friend, but a friend to the Craft. I had talked with him as though he was one of us. I had trusted him. But the fault here was not Ralph's. He was what he was—what he had apparently always been.

The fault was mine.

For being so naive, so careless as to take a mortal into my confidence. To endanger all because I was a credulous, hasty-witted fool.

Ralph was still chatting away as though nothing had changed between us.

"It's a shame these terrible murders had to happen just now. John's bound to be preoccupied. It's all the media seems interested in covering."

But then Ralph didn't know anything had changed between us. He had no idea I was now aware of the existence of the Society for Prevention of Magic in the Mortal Realm. Let alone that I knew—well, suspected—he was a member.

And that was all to the good. Because if Ralph still believed I was clueless, I could feed him false information and he would accept it as truth and hopefully pass it along to his fellow conspirators.

"Yes, terrible," I said automatically. I was afraid my doubt and suspicion were right there on my face for him to read.

Also, I couldn't help wondering what stories Ralph thought the media *should* focus on?

"Valenti tells me she had lunch with you and John's sister on Friday. What did you think of her?"

"She's beautiful," I said. "So, is it serious between the two of you?"

Ralph looked a little taken aback at this uncharacteristic nosiness on my part, but I remembered that the best defense was a good offense. That's not one of the Precepts; I learned it at Krav Kids back in the day.

His smile was rueful. "A delightful girl, but you know me. I'm a confirmed bachelor."

I chuckled. "That used to be code for gay."

"In my case it's code for middle-aged bachelor used to having my own way for far too long." He was still smiling, still genial as he added, "I was happy to hear you turned down the idea of resuming practice."

I was momentarily confused, then remembered the invitation that had turned out not to be an invitation. "Was it a test?" I was still smiling too.

His eyes narrowed. "A test? I'm not sure I understand."

"Was she testing me to see if I was truly worthy?"

Ralph smiled, his flare of unease forgotten. "Oh, I'm sure she's aware what a coup it would be to have the heir to the *trône de sorcière* as her novice."

Yeah, no doubt. And the fucking arrogance! But I continued to smile, as John would have put it, *blithely*.

Ralph grew serious. "I understand you went to visit Ciara Reitherman in jail?"

Despite the phrasing, it wasn't really a question. Or at least, that wasn't his real question.

"She asked for my help. She believes Seamus's murder may be connected to these Witch Killer slayings."

Of course, Ciara didn't believe any such thing, but I thought the idea was worth throwing out there.

Ralph looked flabbergasted. "She believes... That's..."

"Well, it makes sense in a way."

"But it doesn't," he said.

"You don't think there are worrying similarities in these cases?"

"Of course not. *What* similarities? She must be trying to throw suspicion elsewhere. She *had* to have killed Seamus."

He seemed so genuinely startled, so genuinely confused—and alarmed—I wondered if I'd been jumping to *way* too many conclusions.

Blanche joined us then, balancing a stack of much-handled books. "Mr. Grindlewood. How nice to see you again!"

Ralph responded gallantly, if a little by rote, all the while his blue gaze returning to mine, then falling away, as though he couldn't quite believe what he'd heard.

Shortly after, he excused himself.

"Was it something I said?" Blanche remarked as we watched him striding swiftly back toward the shady street crowded with parked cars.

"Possibly something I said. Show me what you found." I leaned over to study the spines on the stack of books she held.

I groaned. "Uh-oh. Tell me these aren't all of the *His Bonnie Highland Captive* ilk…"

* * * * *

Our cocktail party was supposed to start at seven, so I'd left Blue Moon at four thirty, planning to make a stop along the way.

Even from the street, it was clear Oliver was home.

The windows were open, the sheers pushed back, and I could hear the whistle of a teakettle and music—"Danse Macabre" by Camille Saint-Saëns—floating on the summer breeze.

I jogged up the red stone steps, pushed through the short black-and-yellow wrought-iron gate, went up more steps, and rapped briskly on the red-and-yellow door of the small Victorian.

The teakettle's peal cut off, and a moment later the door swung open. Oliver blinked up at me. I saw the impulse to close the door go through his eyes, but then he smiled brightly.

"Cosmo, dear boy! This is an unexpected pleasure!"

Though not such a pleasure that he invited me inside.

"Oliver, when did you get back?"

"Back? Oh. Er… Yesterday. Or no. No, it was Friday, I believe." He smiled at me, blinking all the while like a mole dragged from its hole into scalding sunlight.

"But where did you go?"

"Go? Oh, you know. I was called out of town."

"Called…" I was literally dumbfounded. "I was afraid something happened to you."

"T-to *me*?"

"Yes, to you. We were supposed to meet the night you came to my rehearsal dinner. For two weeks I've been imagining… I'm not even sure!"

Oliver gave a nervous giggle. "No, no. Just a family emergency. I didn't realize you believed we had made an actual appointment."

"But we did. We agreed to meet at the Creaky Attic and look for the—" I stopped even as Oliver put his hand on my arm in caution.

He said, smiling that almost manic smile, "It's all water under the bridge now, isn't it?"

"Is it?" Meeting his gaze, I said doubtfully, "Yes. I suppose it is."

Had I got it wrong all this time? I tried to think back to the night of the rehearsal dinner. So much had happened since then. And a lot of it that very evening. Not impossible to believe some of the details were fuzzy, and yet I vividly remembered standing in the stairwell at the City Club, arranging to meet Oliver at one o'clock that morning. I remembered the jewel-like glow of the colors in Diego Rivera's fresco *Allegory of California*, the tall silhouettes of our shadows against the wall, and the sheen of perspiration on Oliver's forehead.

He had been scared to death.

It occurred to me that he was still scared to death.

I said slowly, "Well, Oliver, I'm very glad you're all right, and the family too, I hope?"

He looked blank for an instant and then gave another of those nervous titters. "Yes, yes! Everyone's fine. No need to worry about the Sandhurst clan."

"Right. Well."

Since he wasn't asking any questions about how it had gone the night I'd searched the Creaky Attic alone, presumably he knew how it had all turned out. Presumably that was what *It's all water under the bridge now* meant. But *how* did he know?

Oliver continued to gaze up at me with those glassy eyes.

"Then it's merry meet, merry part," I said with forced lightness.

"Merry meet again," Oliver finished.

I turned away and started down the steps. As I reached the little black-and-yellow wrought-iron gate, he called suddenly, "Cosmo?"

I turned.

"Take care, dear boy." His gaze seemed oddly intense. "*Do* take care!"

I nodded and turned away.

* * * * *

The best thing about a cocktail party is, in my humble opinion, the cocktails.

Not that I *mind* wine. John was teaching me all kinds of appreciation for good wine—in fact, I now knew what good wine was. But for flavor and variety and quality of inebriation, you just can't beat spirits poured over ice and shaken into submission.

"I had no idea you were such a wizard with a cocktail shaker," John commented as I practiced my warm-up routine that evening.

I removed the lid from the shaker and poured out the frothy concoction of black vodka, cherry juice, orange juice, and maraschino-cherry syrup into a glass with a pinch of pearl dust.

"Would you like one?"

He shuddered. "God no. That thing's half sugar."

"I can do something less sweet. Maybe something champagne-based. How about a classic Death in the Afternoon?"

"What's that have in it?"

I smiled brightly. "Basically, champagne and absinthe."

"Yeah, I don't think so."

I shrugged.

John's brows knotted. "Everything okay?"

"Sure." I winked at him. Sipped from my martini glass. "Perfect."

I meant the drink, but John looked relieved.

"You know, you really do look… amazing," he said for the second time in half an hour. He said it a little helplessly, like he wasn't exactly sure what I was doing there.

"Thank you. Again," I said.

I was wearing a teal, tight-fitting Hugo suit. And my signet ring, bracelets, and amulet. I was pretty sure no one at John's party—our party—well, no, really, John's party—would look like me.

But then no one at our party would *be* like me. Our guests were all John's friends. Or rather, John's colleagues and work relations. San Francisco's movers and shakers. Bureaucrats. Mortals.

It didn't matter. All that mattered was John.

John was wearing navy Italian micro-plaid dress slacks that emphasized the taut, toned beauty of his ass, and a blue, rust, and white multiprint Robert Graham sport shirt with the sleeves rolled to reveal his tanned, muscular forearms.

He looked handsome, successful, rich, powerful—all the things he wanted to look. All the things he was.

I offered, "You look amazing too. I wish…"

I didn't finish it, and he said, "What?"

I shook my head.

I was in a weird mood, no question. Between my encounter with Ralph, my encounter with Oliver, and, to be honest, my… encounter? with John the night before, I was not feeling my usual sanguine self.

In fact, I was worried and afraid, and it was doubly troubling that I couldn't talk to John about any of it. But I had promised him to stay out of it. All of it. Even without either of us knowing what *it* was.

And that wasn't John's fault. It definitely wasn't his fault that I couldn't tell him what was really going on.

I didn't resent John, but I did resent the situation.

John said suddenly, "Cos?"

I raised my eyebrows.

"I promise you, next weekend will be different. No going into the office, no parties, just you and me at home. We can hang pictures or sort our sock drawers or do whatever *you* want. How does that sound?"

"That sounds great. Well, maybe not the sorting socks part." I tossed back the rest of my drink. "I should help Bridget with the hors d'oeuvres."

"Isn't that why we have Bridget?" John asked. "To take care of things like hors d'oeuvres?"

I smiled, shook my head, and went to join Bridget in the kitchen, where it turned out she had everything under control without any help from me.

I mean really. How sad was it that I'd rather hang out in the kitchen with my mother's double agent than with my own husband?

"Mr. Saville, you should leave that to me," Bridget warned as I began to spoon caviar onto the tartlets. "You don't want to be getting anything on that fine suit of yours."

"You must have a spe-home remedy for that."

She sniffed disapprovingly, ignoring the slip. "Besides, it's too soon. Your guests aren't here. These have to be served immediately."

I stepped back from the island counter and raised my hands in surrender. "All right. You win."

She sighed. "If you want to be of use, you can get the bread from the refrigerator."

I got the bread from the refrigerator, set it on the marble counter. "Bridget, how long have you known Nola—"

The doorbell rang, and the microwave exploded.

Yes. You read that right.

I yelped and jumped away from the burning microwave.

Bridget pointed at the blazing appliance. "*Quae mando tibi ille ignis de*."

The flames died. The microwave gave a final sullen crackle and went dark.

Bridget and I stared at each other.

So much for disguises.

She directed a look of pure exasperation at me. "If you *please*, sir?"

"It's not my fault," I protested.

"*Out*," Bridget said.

"I'm going!"

"What just happened?" John asked me, arriving in the doorway in time for us to do an awkward little dance.

I said darkly, "Nothing Bridget can't handle."

He spared a distracted glance over my shoulder. "Our guests are arriving."

I realized for the first time that he was a little on edge about the party. That he needed the evening to go well. That he was not used to throwing parties, not this kind of party. Not the kind of party where the mayor, the police chief, and all the assistant chiefs, deputy chiefs, and rank and file would be rubbing elbows and critiquing the onion dip. They were all an unknown quantity. *I* was an unknown quantity.

I had never known John to be nervous, but he was nervous that night.

And he was right to be.

Chapter Nine

Sergeant Pete Bergamasco didn't like me.

The sergeant was John's aide-cum-one-man-protection-detail-cum-anything-else-John-needed. He was a no-nonsense fifty. Gray hair, gray eyes, gray outlook. Unmarried. In fact, from what I gathered, he had no personal life at all. The job was his life. John was his life.

So maybe it was not a surprise that Bergamasco had not approved of me from the first moment we met. Despite my efforts to charm, greater familiarity had not warmed him to me.

I'd asked John about it once, and John had said something vague about Bergamasco considering me a distraction.

"I'm certainly trying," I'd joked, fluttering my eyelashes. At the time I hadn't taken it seriously.

"What can I get you, Sergeant?" I asked when Bergamasco wandered up to the bar that evening.

By that point, the party was in full swing. I was pulling bartender duty so that John could work the room, and I made sure the drinks were strong and plentiful. Bridget, dressed in a snazzy gray pincord double-breasted housekeeping dress, was circulating with trays of scrumptious nibbles. We were making a good impression. People were impressed. I knew that because although Ella Fitzgerald was scat-singing in the background, it was not so loudly that I couldn't listen in to the conversations flowing around me—which I did, shamelessly.

"Scotch and soda," Bergamasco said crisply, his gaze locked on John, who was courageously bearing up under what appeared to be the double-barreled flattery of both Mayor Stevens's and Chief Morrisey's wives.

"Coming right up." I poured a generous measure of Kilchoman Sauternes Cask Finish, splashed in a little soda, and slid the glass his way. "Have you opened that bottle of twelve-year-old Macallan yet?"

John had also brought Scottish souvenirs back for his staff and friends, though his gifts had leaned heavily toward the liquid.

Bergamasco gave me a dismissive look. "There'll be time for that when we catch these so-called Witch Killers."

"Are you closing in, do you think?"

Deputy Chief Danville, sitting on one of the barstools, cut in, "Then the 'Satanic' motive is still in play?"

"Definitely," the sergeant said. "Both crime scenes had photos, items, and physical evidence suggesting the victims practiced witchcraft."

I refreshed Danville's Chivas Regal. These cops all had two speeds: beer or whisky. Plastered or sober. Boring. But it kept things simple.

"The two aren't necessarily connected," I said.

Danville and Bergamasco looked as blank as if John's unicorn bottle holder had spoken up.

Bergamasco said, "The department has an occult expert. Our expert says—"

I cut in, "Right. John mentioned that. I'm wondering if this expert might be someone I know?"

Danville looked taken aback. Bergamasco glanced at the silver bracelets I wore. His expression was unreadable, but I knew what he was thinking. Bergamasco was no fool.

"Solomon Shimon," he said.

The name meant nothing to me. If I'm honest, I'd been expecting to hear "Ralph Grindlewood" or "Valenti Garibaldi." A name to feed my growing conspiracy theories. Whoever this Shimon person was, he was unknown to me. That didn't necessarily mean he wasn't the real deal, but I was pretty familiar with the Bay Area community of witches and Wiccans. It was hard to believe I'd not have at least heard of someone with enough of a rep to work for SFPD.

"I don't know the name."

Bergamasco brightened at that news. "Shimon works at SF State. He teaches a course on witchcraft and the occult every semester."

I said, "I see. Have you considered speaking to someone within the Wiccan community? An actual participating member of the community?"

"That's the last thing we'd want," Danville said.

"I don't follow."

"That's because you're not a cop," Bergamasco said.

It was tempting to say what I *was*, but I was sure John wouldn't appreciate that.

"So true," I said cheerfully, and began to put together a tray of cocktails.

A few minutes later I made my way through the crowd, offering martini glasses brimming with "the house special."

"These are *gorgeous*," Deputy Chief Danville's wife said, holding one aloft to catch the light. "What are they called?"

"Black Magic martinis."

"What makes them sparkle like that?"

"Wilton Edible Pearl Dust."

"Cosmo, you have a *lovely* home," another woman said. "I can't believe how fast you two have settled in."

"I can't believe how fast they got married," Danville's wife said.

"We had to. I'm pregnant," I said.

We all laughed.

"Have another drink," I invited. They all had another drink.

The conversation turned to the wedding, then back to John and mine's whirlwind courtship, then to the antiques business, then back to John himself. By then the mayor's wife had joined our circle.

"Your husband is *so* sexy," she informed me. "In a totally intimidating way. I always wonder what's going on behind those dark, magnetic eyes."

"Talking about me?" the mayor chimed in, which sent everyone into peals of merriment. Never underestimate the power of Black Magic martinis.

I said, "I'm just hoping these awful Witch Killers are caught soon, so I can spend the occasional evening with him again."

That sobered them up, in a manner of speaking. "Don't we all," the mayor said, shaking his head.

"Has anyone thought of trying to enlist the help of the local Wiccan community?" I suggested.

"Obviously people are being questioned," Mayor Stevens said.

"Right. Of course. I don't know how these things work. But what about approaching members as resources rather than suspects? Has anyone thought about that?"

That raised a few eyebrows, though mostly people were looking at each other and nodding in approval.

"Obviously, I'm not privy to the details of the investigation. The department has its own expert."

"Naturally. The thing is, one woman was a newly anointed High Priestess and the other was an active member of the same coven."

"How would you know that?" Mayor Stevens asked.

"I have friends within the Wiccan community."

A woman—Danville's wife perhaps?—peered at me and gave a little squeal. "Oh my God. I get it now. Are you a *witch*?"

"I don't think that's allowed," I joked.

"No, that's not allowed," John said, joining our group. He was smiling, but his eyes met mine, unamused.

Everyone else was amused, though. Everyone else thought this was all in good fun.

"It's *warlock* for men," Mrs. Morrisey informed them, and they all nodded in knowing agreement.

One of the things I find entertaining about mortals is that— despite the fact they have no magic (or negligible magic)—they have elaborate and convoluted theories, rules, of how magic should work. Needless to say, they get it mostly wrong.

The mayor said, "John, your husband is starting to think like a cop."

"I wouldn't say that," John said.

I chose to ignore the warning in his eyes. I said, "The thing I'm starting to wonder about is whether there could be a connection between these murders and the Seamus Reitherman slaying."

"A connection? How could there be a connection?"

That was Chief Morrisey, who had also now joined our little enclave.

"Oh my God, Harold," Mrs. Morrisey said. "Cosmo is a warlock. It's *so* cute."

"Well, think about it," I said, staring straight into John's forbidding gaze. "Three occult-related murders within the span of a month. If they're *not* related, that's quite a coincidence, don't you think?"

"It is," Mrs. Stevens agreed, and Mrs. Morrisey concurred. The chief, looking completely taken aback, turned to John.

John smiled a Big Bad Wolf sort of smile. "Someone's sure enjoying the cocktails," he said.

"We're *all* enjoying the cocktails," Mrs. Danville replied, reaching for another.

"You're the one who told me there are no such things as coincidences in police work," I said.

"That's not true," Bergamasco replied. Because, yes, now pretty much everyone in the room was paying attention to this conversation. "Coincidences have to be ruled out, but they do occur. Of course they do."

"It can't hurt to double-check, though, right?"

"But the Reitherman case is airtight, isn't it?" the mayor asked the police chief.

"Of course," the chief responded. "It was a domestic dispute that got out of hand. It's a slam dunk."

"I knew both Seamus and Ciara," I said. "It's very hard to believe she'd have anything to do with his death."

"Everybody says that in a murder investigation," the mayor said kindly.

John's sigh was long-suffering. "Nowadays everyone thinks they're a detective. Including my husband."

"It's the TV. Ann is just the same," Chief Morrisey said.

"*Hey*," Mrs. Morrisey protested.

John looped an arm around the chief's shoulders, said, "We brought back a peated single malt you have to try…" and led him off.

And that was that.

Except it wasn't.

It was after eleven when at last the party wound down.

Bridget had already departed, leaving the kitchen spic and span—and how could John not notice, how could he not realize how impossible that was? But of course, John's attention was elsewhere.

He saw out our final guests—one of the assistant chiefs and his wife—closed the door, locked it, and turned to me.

He said quietly, "Are you out of your fucking mind?"

I had known this reckoning was coming. I wasn't looking forward to it, but I knew there was no avoiding it. It wasn't as though a few hours and a couple of drinks would erase the look

I'd seen on John's face when I'd tried to interest the chief and mayor into taking a closer look at the Reitherman investigation.

I said, "I don't think so. No."

"What the hell was that all about?"

"I think there could be a connection between these cases. Does it hurt to take a look?"

"Does it…" He tried again. "I don't understand you. I specifically told you—requested—that you not stick your nose into police business. And you agreed."

"I shouldn't have."

"You…shouldn't…have?"

"No. I shouldn't have. This isn't about you or me. People are dying. I have information that could be useful to the Witch Killer investigation. You care about justice. I would think you'd want that information shared."

"What I want is for you to stay out of police business. How would you feel if I started telling you how to run your shop? Would you feel that maybe I crossed a line?"

"This is a false equivalence, John. I'm not telling you how to do your job. You're not personally investigating this case. I'm pointing out facts that have so far been missed in the investigation. Even if Seamus's murder isn't connected to these others, things are being overlooked. An athame being mistaken for a boline. Two members of the same coven being targeted—"

"You're guessing these things. You don't know them for a fact."

"I know they need to be double-checked. And if you would have listened to me, I wouldn't have felt compelled to take matters into my own hands."

That was the truth, but to say it out loud was probably a mistake. No, it was *definitely* a mistake.

He considered and discarded several responses before saying, tightly, tersely, "I'm not going to tell you again. Do not further embarrass me in front of my colleagues. Stay out of police business. Stay out of *my* business. Do you understand me?"

I'm not sure why that was the breaking point. I had successfully been rationalizing his demands up until then, and he had certainly said worse things to me. But all at once, I'd had enough.

I snapped, "I understand that you have a narrow and bigoted frame of reference."

He shouted, "*Bigoted?* I went ahead and married a kook who thinks he's a goddamned witch."

I yelled back, "I don't *think* I'm a goddamned witch. I *am* a witch."

Chapter Ten

The reverberating silence that followed was even louder than our raised voices.

I was shocked and horrified by what I'd done. Even so, I wouldn't have taken it back even if it had been possible. As sick as I felt, I was—weirdly—almost relieved that it was finally out.

However, it didn't have quite the effect I was expecting.

After a moment, John said dryly, "I see."

Still angry. I matched him, arid syllable for arid syllable. "No, you don't."

You will.

There was malice in that thought. I rejected it at once, ashamed. I was angry and hurt, but I'd die before I hurt John.

His lip curled. "Yeah, I do. Only too well."

"Except you *don't*." I nodded at the amber chandelier, and the light went out.

From the shadows near the front door, John said wearily, "Jesus. You actually *coordinated* this little display?"

I snapped my fingers, and the lights flared back on. "Seriously? You think this is a-a parlor trick?"

"I think this is staged. Hell, yes." His smile was derisive. "Am I now supposed to believe you have magical powers?"

My mouth fell open. I mean, skepticism was one thing. This was... He couldn't *really* think I had...what? Wired the room? Did he honestly believe I was that much of a kook?

I bit out, "*Table rise before his eyes.*"

The peanut dish still sitting on the coffee table rattled as the table in the sunken living room began to rise.

John watched, unmoving and unmoved, as the table rose to the height of the surrounding railing.

As the table hung there in midair, John's gaze flashed to mine. "Land it on the sofa," he ordered.

I looked at the table and pointed to the sofa. The table floated down again and landed lightly on the gray sectional. The peanut dish slipped off the edge and fell to the floor, cracking in half and scattering nuts.

John moved to the railing and stared down at the tableau below us. Coffee table sitting drunkenly on the sofa, broken dish, the peanut-dotted carpet. His face was absolutely expressionless. I could barely see the rise and fall of his chest.

Finally, he looked me square in the face. "Move the brass bed upstairs down here."

I glanced overhead and then toward the dining room. "There's not enough room."

His voice was as hard as the *crack* of gavel. "Move it."

"As you wish," I said haughtily.

But it had been a long time since I'd tried to move anything large or complicated.

Bed appear

Right over here.

Nothing.

I closed my eyes, picturing our bed, and whispered, "*Frame speculum sphærulæque per singulos, et ex aere fabricabis, per tempus moveri per spatia. Hie mihi copulare.*"

Nothing happened.

I said more firmly, "*Frame speculum sphærulæque per singulos, et ex aere fabricabis, per tempus moveri per spatia. Hie mihi copulare.*"

Nothing.

"This is embarrassing," John said.

I ignored him, taking a step forward and staring at the ceiling. I concentrated with all my might. My heart sped up, sweat broke out on my forehead. "*Frame speculum sphærulæque per singulos, et ex aere fabricabis, per tempus moveri per spatia. Hic mihi copulare.*"

The amber chandelier near the door began to swing. The bed appeared in the open walkway between the dining room and the living room. The image wavered, faded, and then the bed settled, knocking over a side table, pushing hard against the living room railing, which groaned and bent beneath the pressure.

John stared at the bent railing, stared at the bed. He said nothing. I've seen statues show more emotion.

"You don't think this is something you should have mentioned earlier?" he said at last.

Some of my defiance faded. "I… It's forbidden."

"You're telling me now."

"You're my-my beloved consort now. I didn't want this between us."

His hawkish gaze flickered at that. "I see."

I wondered uneasily if I had short-circuited his brain. I said, "You saw my collection of grimoires. You knew I—"

He said harshly, "You know goddamned well I had no idea of *this*."

I flinched.

"What else can you do?"

"I don't understand."

"What's the full extent of your…your powers?"

I faltered. "I… I mean, that's not an easy question to answer. I try not to use—"

"Can you fly on a broomstick?"

I said, "I… It's just… Why would I want to?"

"Can you?"

"Yes, I guess I could." I also guess I could have explained that broom riding was an early exercise to teach children control and balance, but was not—and had never been—a normal means of transportation. I mean, who wants to smack into a bird or get bugs in their teeth and hair if they don't have to?

"Do you use a cauldron?"

"For what? Making soup? I use the same Cuisinart stainless-steel cookware you do."

"Have you used magic on me?"

I swallowed.

He repeated in a voice as cold and relentless as a Highland winter, "Answer the question. Have you tried to control me with magic?"

I said quickly, "No. No, it wasn't like that."

"You're lying. I told you, never lie to me." As he said it, his face changed, grew even more frightening as he remembered. "The night of our rehearsal dinner…when you tried…" His gaze grew bright and hostile. "You were trying to cast a spell on me?"

"I wasn't trying to control you. It was never for my own gain."

"You used *magic* on *me*?"

I moved my head in assent. "I'm sorry. It was wrong. I knew it was wrong. I was…desperate."

Desperate not to lose you. I managed not to say it, but it was the truth. I saw that now. At the time I had tried to tell myself I had to protect the Abracadantès; in fact, the whole consortium of witchdom. I had reassured myself it was for both our sakes, but no. I had done it for myself. If I had really had the best interests of witchdom at heart, I'd have called off the wedding.

I'm not sure he even heard me.

"And that wasn't the first time. You did something earlier that day, after you faint—" He stopped, and I could see him trying to remember. No, not *trying*. He *was* remembering.

My heart sped up with genuine alarm as I saw the final confirmation of what I'd suspected for a while: that when John consciously exerted his will, he could throw off the effects of magic. Weeks later, he was brushing off the fragile remnants of that first forgetting spell.

The old wives' tales about witch hunters were true. Some of them could even resist or overcome magic.

"You didn't faint," he said. "You were hit by a piano falling out of…nowhere."

"I—yes. That was Ciara. She believed I killed Seamus, and she was trying to avenge him. She didn't realize you were there, of course. She's reckless, but not that reckless. She wouldn't have—that's why I know she's innocent…"

I recognized that I was babbling to fill the dreadful silence between us, and shut up.

John stared at me like he was seeing me for the first time.

Which, I suppose, he was.

"How did I end up marrying you?" For the record, that wasn't an insult; it was a sincere question.

"You weren't—aren't—under a spell." The temptation to leave it there almost undermined my courage, but I couldn't fail him this time. I made myself say, "I had it removed the morning after Seamus was murdered."

Something terrifying crossed his face. Emotion turned his eyes yellow, and he said thickly, "*You*—" and stepped toward me.

"*It wasn't me.*"

He looked like he hated me. For one moment, I truly thought he would kill me. I stumbled back, crying out, "*Transcendet ostium, ut iubes.*"

I had wondered how it could be that such an old house had no postern, and I saw now that the doorway predated the house. Latin turned the key.

I fell through and landed several blocks away.

For a time I knelt there panting, sick, in a triangle of lamplight.

I hadn't been wrong to tell John the truth. I had been wrong in the way I did it. I had blurted it out in anger and frustration, and of course he was shocked. Of course he did not understand.

I did not blame him. I blamed myself.

Which did not change the fact that I was afraid of him. Afraid to go back.

The minutes passed. A bus rumbled past. I grew calmer. The night air cooled the perspiration on my face and body. I listened to the chirping of crickets, the distant city sounds.

Anyway, what was I going to do? Hide in the bushes? Huddle in a bus stop all night? I *had* to go home. I had to face John.

We had to talk.

I closed my eyes, thinking of his face in those final moments.

But no.

He loved me. He would not hurt me. I believed that. However angry he had been, he wouldn't have harmed me. Not really.

I shivered. The night felt cold now.

Turning toward Greenwich Street, I hiked back and knocked on the door of our house.

The porch light came on, and the door opened. John stood framed in the amber light of the chandelier. I could see at once that the rage had passed.

I said huskily, "May I come in?"

He opened the door the rest of the way, moved back.

I stepped inside. "John, I—"

He put up a hand, and I stopped mid-word.

"I've already worked it out. Andi cast the…spell."

I swallowed. I wouldn't willingly expose Andi to what I'd seen in John's eyes fifteen minutes earlier.

But I didn't need to confirm or deny; he did already know the truth and had moved on. "And it was after you found out and, I suppose, told her to lift the enchantment, that you made this phone call." He pulled his phone out, impatiently flicked the screen a few times, then held the phone out for me to listen to the message.

"Hey," my tinny voice quavered with stress and emotion. My swallow was audible, and so was the struggle to steady my voice. *"I just wanted to say...I love you. I always will. Meeting you..."* It sounded like I'd suddenly stepped into a wind tunnel—or was about to keel over. My lifetime-ago-self gulped out, *"...changed my life. Whatever happens, I'm never going to regret that. I just...thought you should know."*

John snapped off the recording. He smiled, and the smile was almost worse than what I'd seen in his eyes before I'd fled the house. "I actually saved this message. That whole never-ending hell of a week, every time I thought, *No, you didn't bargain for this*, I'd play that message and feel so sure it was right. That what was between us was special."

"John—"

He laughed, and tears burned my eyes. "I was right. There *is* something special about you. I just thought it was something good."

I wiped my eyes. I didn't know what to say. I didn't know what I *could* say.

"*Now* it all begins to make sense." He was thinking aloud, talking to himself. I just happened to be there.

I looked past him and saw two suitcases sitting at the bottom of the staircase.

My heart stopped. My lungs wouldn't work for an instant.

I finally managed a winded, "Are you leaving?"

John made a sound of disbelief. "What did you have in mind? Marriage counseling?

I put my hand out, dimly registering the pain when he stepped out of reach.

I said, "We could talk. You could let me explain. There's another side to this."

"I'm sure there is. I don't want to hear it. Every minute of this relationship was a lie. Worse than a lie."

"It *wasn't*. John, please—*please* listen to me."

"If you'd wanted me to listen, you should have tried talking to me before we married."

I winced.

He gave another of those unpleasant smiles. "You made quite a fool out of me."

"*No,*" I denied, pained.

"Oh, hell yes. Sure you did. Tonight alone…"

"John, please believe me. I love you." I rushed on, trying not to see his expression, that mingled look of disgust and disbelief. "I know you're angry, and you have a right to be. I didn't mean to hurt you. I'd never knowingly harm you. Maybe I should have called off the wedding. I should have. I see that now. But I had come to believe you really did love me."

That, and he'd had plenty of practical reasons for marrying me. He had spelled them out for me in this very room.

"You *love* me?" John repeated incredulously. "Is that what that was? That's you in love? What would be left to do to someone you *didn't* love?"

"If you'd just give me a chance to explain." Not that I could think of a single thing to say that might change his mind. "It's more complicated than you think."

"No, it isn't," he said with finality. "This part isn't. The time to explain was *before* we married. Although later would have been better than *never*, which was apparently your plan."

"No. I *was* going to tell you. I knew I had to tell you. I wasn't sure how. You wouldn't have believed me. I was waiting for the right moment."

"For future reference, the visual aids go a long way to making your point." He turned, went to the staircase, and picked up his suitcases.

"Please don't do this."

He ignored me, heading for the front door.

I faltered. "But where will you go? How will I reach you?"

"I don't want you to reach me." He opened the door.

I could have slammed it shut again. I could have prevented him from leaving. Maybe I couldn't insist he talk to me, but I could have forced him to listen.

I did none of that, of course. Only stood there shaking and sick and afraid.

"Please don't go. John. Please don't walk away."

He didn't even look at me.

I followed him out into the vestibule, still pleading. "I'm the same person I was in Scotland. I'm still...it's still me."

He did glance at me then. "Is it? Maybe. The problem is, I don't know who that is. I never did. And now I don't want to."

Chapter Eleven

Obviously, I'm not the first witch to marry a mortal.

I'm not even the first witch in my family. In fact, the prevailing theory as to why Great-great-great-uncle Arnold, er, *dispatched* Great-great-great-aunt Esmerelda is that she was mortal.

Marrying mortals is not forbidden, but it is strongly discouraged.

And should the relationship go wrong, it's naturally up to the witch to make sure no harm is done. Meaning, make sure the Craft does not pay the price for one's romantic indiscretions.

Usually that can be accomplished through a forgetting spell.

But in John's case, application of a forgetting spell was not possible, which is why as morning drew near, I stopped feeling sorry for myself and started worrying about John.

Not that I really believed John was in danger, but once word got out that he'd left me, there would certainly be concern in various quarters, and one of those quarters would be the Société du Sortilège.

The fact that John was a policeman—well, no, worse, the police commissioner—would undoubtedly trigger all kinds of paranoia. It was up to me to reassure everyone who mattered that John did not pose a threat to me or the Craft.

I hoped it was true.

The first thing I did after arriving at Blue Moon on Monday morning was try to phone John at City Hall.

It was a relief to hear from Pat that he was in the office and working. It was less of a relief to learn he wouldn't take my call.

Pat said apologetically, "I'm sorry, Mr. Saville, he's on the other line."

"I'll hold."

She said, with just a shade of discomfort, "The commissioner said not to."

"Oh. Then… Could you…" I faltered.

Pat said kindly, firmly, "I'll let him know you'd like him to return your call."

Yes. To put it mildly.

John did not return my phone call.

I tried his cell phone a few times as the hours dragged on, but the calls went straight to message. I suspected he had blocked me.

I knew it would be best to let him cool down, give him time to think, to maybe even miss me a little. Even so, I had to fight with myself all morning long not to keep phoning.

Phone? Ha. I could make it impossible for him to ignore me and simply appear in his office.

But no. It was not just the possibility of materializing in the middle of a meeting that stopped me. I knew instinctively that the more I tried to bend John to my will, the stronger his resistance to me would grow.

Why, *why* had I done it? Why had I told him the truth—and in such a way? *Why* couldn't I have kept my mouth shut?

The more I agonized over my foolishness, the more I wondered if in some dark corner of my subconsciousness, I had wanted this outcome. Well, no. I hadn't wanted *this* outcome. But maybe secretly I'd allowed the argument with John to escalate so I could tell myself I had no choice but to reveal the truth to him.

If so, I'd seriously miscalculated.

Granted, I hadn't expected him to take the truth well. I'd known there was always the risk it would change what he felt for me. When I'd been feeling particularly insecure, I'd relied on his pragmatism. His numerous practical reasons for wanting to marry me were still in place. If anything, I'd worried he might see a useful side to my gifts.

Lunchtime came and went with no word from John.

I did my best to focus on work.

Late afternoon, distraction came in the form of a surprise visit from Ralph Grindlewood.

"Can we speak in private?" Ralph asked with an apologetic glance at Ambrose and Blanche.

"Of course." I led the way into my office.

Ralph took the Erwin-Lambeth plum velvet Neo-Chippendale wing chair as he had done so often in the past. He smiled. "We've been friends a long while now, haven't we?"

I said, "I always thought so."

"And friends should be frank with each other, don't you think?"

"Sure."

"As you know, I admire your decision to renounce a life of magic and live as a mortal. Your decision to marry John seemed to me to cement that resolve. Which is why I'm a little dismayed now to learn you've begun to involve yourself in things that are, to be blunt, no longer your concern."

I raised my brows. "What things?"

"The activities of the Society for Prevention of Magic in the Mortal Realm."

It wasn't a shock—I had suspected Ralph's involvement since my wedding—but it was unexpected to hear him simply admit it like that.

When I didn't react, Ralph tilted his head. "Surely you're not going to pretend you don't know what I'm talking about?"

"No."

"Are you going to deny that you've been meddling?"

You meddling kids!

"Something funny?" Ralph frowned.

"To be honest, you sound a little like a *Scooby-Doo* villain. What is it you want me to do? Or rather, not do?"

Ralph's smile returned. "Your appreciation of mortal culture is one of the more endearing things about you. To begin with, stop playing detective. These so-called Witch Killer murders are not in any way connected to Seamus Reitherman's tragic death."

I tried not to let my disquiet show. The only possible way Ralph could have learned that I was pushing for the police to connect Seamus's death with the Witch Killer murders was if someone at last night's party had reported it to him. Hard as it was to believe, someone in City Hall's upper echelon had to be a member of SPMMR.

"How do you know?" I asked at last.

"I know," Ralph said. "And I want to remind you that even if these crimes *were* connected, that would not be your concern."

I said, "I'll decide what matters relating to the Craft are my concern, Ralph."

He studied me over his long, steepled fingers and then nodded thoughtfully. "Spoken like the young Duc of Westlands. But I don't think that job description is compatible with being the husband of San Francisco's police commissioner, do you?"

"*Qui vivra verra.*"

"Mm… Perhaps I can ease your conscience. SPMMR is not in any way involved in these crimes. We are a nonviolent organization."

I didn't answer, as yet another worrying question arose. How had Ralph come to know of my interest in the Society for Prevention of Magic in the Mortal Realm? The only person I'd discussed my concerns with was Andi. Well, and Maman. Both were above suspicion.

"I see," I said.

"Do you?"

"I'm not sure I believe you, but I do understand what you're telling me."

"Let me clarify further. It could prove hazardous to your health if you continue poking your nose into what doesn't concern you."

I smiled. "Are you threatening me?"

"*No.* I most certainly am not. Of all members of the Société du Sortilège, your sympathies align most closely with ours. No one at SPMMR regards you as an enemy. There is concern that your meddling—"

"That word again."

"Might bring you to the attention of someone dangerous. Someone who does not see you as a possible ally."

I stared. "Ralph, if you know who's behind these crimes, you need to speak up."

He rose. "I've said all I intend to."

I rose too. "You *do* know who's murdering these women!" I was genuinely horrified.

Ralph's expression remained impassive.

"You can't permit this to go on. If this person isn't part of your organization—"

"Of course not. It's nothing to do with us. And it's nothing to do with you. Stay out of it, Cosmo. I say this as your friend." He headed for the door. Hand on the knob, he stopped. "One other thing. John's sister. Joan."

"What about her?"

"Valenti has taken the girl under her wing. Please don't attempt to derail that friendship."

"Or what?" I asked.

Ralph shrugged. "Or there will be hurt feelings all around." He added, "And someone may feel it necessary to inform John about who and what you really are."

I laughed.

"I'm not joking, unfortunately."

"And I'm not worried."

After a moment he nodded and went out of the office.

Near the end of the day, my cell phone finally rang.

I snatched it up, but to my disappointment, the caller was my mother. In fairness, it was not entirely disappointing to see Maman's symbol flash up, as I did urgently need to speak with her.

I clicked to answer, and she said, "Cosmo, why have you been harassing Phelon? Is it so impossible you two could get along like adults in my absence?"

"Where in the name of the Goddess have you *been*?"

She said a little huffily, "*J'ai profité d'un peu de temps au spa.* If you must know."

"With everything going on right now?" I cried.

"What is it that's going on?"

"*Ugh.* I'll see you in five."

Three minutes later I stepped into the library of my mother's Nob Hill mansion. She was seated before the fireplace, pouring tea from a blue-and-gold Aynsley teapot.

She glanced up. "Come and have your tea, *mon chou.* What is all this drama, if you please?"

I kissed her cheek, took the proffered teacup, and proceeded to relate all the drama. Maman listened without interrupting, only the smallest frown marring the marble perfection of her forehead.

According to my aunts and uncles, I look like my mother. Same willowy height, same milky skin, same wavy dark hair. Her eyes are green, mine are gray, but yes, in looks we are similar. In other ways…not so much.

Which isn't to say we aren't close. We are. Occasionally, we even see eye to eye. Maman, that is, Estelle Saville, Duchesse d'Abracadantès, is many things. At fifty, she is beautiful, charming (when she chooses), well-educated, often wise, and frequently ruthless. She plays piano beautifully, has spent the last five years working on translating the memoirs of the witch Françoise-Athénaïs de Rochechouart, Marquise de Montespan, and still gives fencing lessons (which is where she hooked up with the objectionable Phelon Penn, her current companion). What she is not and has never been is unduly—or at all—concerned with the affairs of mortals. Including Wiccans.

"How is this any of our affair?" she asked when I had finally come to the end of my recital.

I spluttered, "Seamus wasn't a Wiccan. Seamus was one of us."

She shrugged. "True, I suppose. But you don't know for certain that these crimes are connected. This former friend of yours insists they are not."

I winced at the former-friend comment. John was one thing. Those indiscretions could be overlooked. But it was painful to think how I'd confided in Ralph over the years.

Although, in my defense, I hadn't told him anything he didn't already know. I had certainly confirmed a few facts, though.

"I don't think we can trust anything Ralph said."

"No? You believe he was lying?"

I was silent, pondering. I was forced to admit, "No. I think he was telling the truth."

"*Eh bien.*" She sipped her tea. "Why are you so sure Seamus's murder is connected to these others? They don't seem anything alike to me."

"I'm not sure. Or at least I wasn't. But the fact that Ralph seems convinced he knows who the killer is makes me think it must be someone mortal. Or else how would he know?"

"Hmm…"

"When I found Seamus, there was no scintilla, so the killer could well be mortal."

"It isn't much to go on."

"I know." I stared at the dregs in my teacup and set the cup on the table. "You haven't said anything about the rest of it. About John."

"Ah, yes. John," Maman said wearily. "Descended from witch hunters. *Ça explique beaucoup.*"

"Did you hear anything else I said?"

She arched an eyebrow. "You mean, did I grasp the fact that John has left you?"

I looked away, biting my lip. "Yes."

"Of course. It hardly comes as a surprise, since I predicted this from the outset."

I said bitterly, "I haven't forgotten."

She made a small exasperated sound. "Come, *mon fils chéri.* It's not as if I had any hand in his betrayal. I can't say I'm sorry to have him out of our lives. Especially with this new information regarding his loathsome ancestry." She shook her head, as though even now the thought of my foolishness stumped her.

I dropped my face in my hands. "I don't want to talk about it."

"I'm relieved to know the last forty-five minutes were merely a bad dream."

I lowered my hands, glared.

"The question that remains is what do you think he will do with his newfound knowledge?"

"Nothing."

Her smothered laugh was derisive.

"Nothing. He doesn't pose a threat to any of us."

"I hope not."

"It's not even for sure that our marriage is over."

"Oh, Cosmo." She seemed truly sorry for me, which was alarming.

"It's not. Once he calms down, once we have a chance to talk, he may… It may be all right."

She made a pained sound, though less sympathetic and more exasperated.

"I'm not ready to give up," I said. "I think he still loves me. I still love him."

"Épargnez-moi, s'il te plaît. Now, as for your request that I approach la Société du Sortilège regarding these murders. *Non.*"

I sat up straight. "What? *Why?*"

She was brisk. "It would be preferable for you to go yourself, Cosmo. You have not spoken directly with your great-aunt since before your marriage. You chose not to ask her permission to marry a mortal. It is the least you can do to inform her of the risk to all of us now posed by this man."

My great-aunt was Laure d'Estrées, currently Crone or the Abracadantès Queen of Witches. A real Witch Queen, not, like Valenti, a self-appointed ruler.

It was true that due to the fluke of my position on the line of ascension, correct protocol required my asking permission to marry anyone, let alone a mortal. I had not done so. I'd informed Great-aunt Laure over the phone that I was going to marry John, and that had been that.

She had taken it well. In fact, she had sent us a 19th century wedding armoire with carved lovebirds, flowers, and acanthus leaves as a wedding gift.

"But the murders have nothing to do with my marriage. This is a threat to all witchdom."

"Perhaps there is no connection. Perhaps there is. How can you know? In any case, you are Duc of Westlands. These problems and challenges are as much yours as anyone's. And, after all, you are the one with all the theories."

I didn't like it, but she was right.

I sighed. "All right. I'll go to Paris."

She refilled my teacup. We sipped our tea in silence.

She said finally, "Has it occurred to you that what most attracted you to John was his infatuation with you?"

Yes, actually, it had occurred to me once or twice. I had blocked it out, of course, because…well, because.

Because having insisted on going through with our marriage, it was unbearable to think I had been as deluded as John.

"No."

She arched a single eyebrow. "The John you fell in love with was a man bewitched, *n'est-ce pas*? It was not the real man. Not the man in his right mind. In that sense, you were both under a spell."

"Even so—"

"Even so, is there not something seductive about winning over someone who first seems unwinnable?"

"No."

"But of course there is. What is it your Groucho Marx would say? 'I don't want to belong to any club that would accept me as one of its members.' You were wounded when John did not want you as a member of his club, and won over once he did."

I stared at her in astonishment. Not least because I had no idea she'd ever heard of Groucho Marx, let alone knew I'd watched every Marx Brothers movie during my teens.

"No," I said again. "*C'est ridicule.*" I had certainly had boyfriends through the years, certainly people had fallen in love with me, but no one had swept me off my feet the way John had. And yes, probably some of that was the feeling of conquest.

"*Je ne suis pas si sûre.* After all, you're used to being catered to, flattered, wooed by men you fear are more entranced by your wealth and title than yourself. I have heard you say this more than once. How irritating and yet refreshing it must have been to meet someone genuinely not impressed. And how… *séduisant* when you were able to win him over."

I protested, "It wasn't at all like that!"

"Wasn't it?"

"No! It wasn't."

And yet…

She was right in that the first John I'd fallen in love with had been more fantasy than flesh and blood. A dream lover. Romantic and passionate and attentive to the point of noting my every change of expression. Willing to do anything and everything for me, regardless of his normal feelings and attitudes. In all honesty, it probably would have gotten tiresome eventually, but at the time…

Looking at it now, I could see—unwillingly—that it was possible there was some truth to what my mother suggested.

There *had* been something seductive about knowing someone as hard and unyielding as John, someone who had initially resisted me, was so completely smitten.

I said, "But this is true of all relationships, isn't it? Everyone falls in love with a stranger. It's once you come to know the person that you learn whether love is true. Even after the spell was lifted, even after I came to know the real John, I did still—I do still—love him."

True. That part was true. I was reassured by the thought.

She cocked her head, considering. "But even now, you've only known each other a few weeks."

"It doesn't matter."

"No? Well, you know best. However, it is my belief you were in love with John being in love with you. And now you are beginning to wake from that spell."

"You're wrong."

She shrugged, and echoing what I'd told Ralph earlier, I said, "Time will tell."

Chapter Twelve

Maybe I wasn't such a bad detective after all, because it didn't take me long to figure out where John was spending the night.

Sure enough, his Range Rover was parked on the street in front of Sergeant Bergamasco's bungalow.

Lights shined behind the window blinds, and I could hear the sound of a televised baseball game as I walked up to the front door. My mouth was dry, my heart skipping as I rang the doorbell. I felt cold and sick, and I wasn't even sure why.

The worst he could do was refuse to speak to me, and why would he? We were both grown-ups. We could surely talk this out like reasonable adults.

Okay, yes, I can't deny that I was a little worried about what John might have told Bergamasco. I didn't believe he would tell the sergeant the complete truth, though I wasn't one hundred percent sure. That's what a lifetime of paranoia regarding mortals will do to you. John would have to tell Bergamasco something, though, and it probably wasn't that our house was being fumigated or that I had been placed in quarantine, even if last night he'd probably have been in favor of either option.

I was just about to ring the doorbell again when the porch light came on. I heard the lock turn, and the door swung open.

Sergeant Bergamasco stood before me in gray sweatpants and a red T-shirt that read: *Stones No Filter Tour 2019*. I'd never seen him out of his uniform of suit and tie.

"Hi, Sergeant," I said. "Is— May I speak to John?"

Bergamasco said awkwardly, "I'm sorry, Mr. Saville. The commissioner isn't…" It wasn't in him to lie, so he just stopped.

I'd told myself I was braced for it, but I really wasn't. It took me a second to find my voice. "Sergeant, please. If you could just…" I broke off as Bergamasco began to shake his head.

"Can I give you some advice, Mr. Saville? Let him cool down. He's not in a good frame of mind right now."

"And I know that's good advice," I said quickly, hoping if I got the words out fast, my voice wouldn't shake. "The problem is, I have some information regarding these murders—"

I broke off as Bergamasco threw a quick look over his shoulder and stepped out onto the front step, half closing the door behind him.

He kept his voice low. "Look, I don't know what went down last night between you and the commissioner. But I do know he was mad as hell during the party when you started going around insisting we ought to be interviewing High Priestesses, and then telling the mayor our occult expert is getting things wrong."

As much as I wanted to avoid further antagonizing anyone at City Hall, I couldn't help replying, "Do you care about solving these murders, or do you only care about how things look?"

Bergamasco sucked in a deep breath. He said evenly, "Mr. Saville, I know you're upset. I know this is rough on you too. But this is not the way to get back in the commissioner's good graces."

"*His good graces?*"

"Okay, this is not the way to get his attention, if you prefer."

"What I'd prefer is actually speaking to my husband."

Bergamasco said grimly, "You think *I* wouldn't prefer that too?"

My shoulders slumped as my righteous indignation drained away. "I'm sure you would. Look, I'm sorry to put you in the

middle. Could you… Could you ask John again? Could you tell
him I'm *begging* him to give me five minutes? That's all. Just
five minutes."

Bergamasco hesitated, sighed, and went inside.

I didn't even have time to get my hopes up. He was back a
moment later, shaking his head.

"He won't see you," Bergamasco said. "I'm sorry. He says
go home. He'll let you know when he's ready to talk."

He waited a moment, watching me with a glimmer of un-
willing sympathy as I stood motionless, absorbing it, and then
he quietly, almost softly, closed the front door.

I listened to the *buzz* of the porch light, the soft battering
of moths hitting the glass, and then I turned and walked down
the steps.

* * * * *

"That's the other risk of telling them. What if they can't
accept us for who we are?" Andi murmured sympathetically.

It was Tuesday afternoon, and we were having lunch at a
little café not far from the Mad Batter.

I nodded wearily. I had not slept the night before. I could
not imagine ever falling asleep again with that great stretch of
empty mattress next to me.

"Have you ever used magic on Trace?"

She shook her head.

"No, of course not." I expelled a long sigh and pressed the
heels of my hands to my eyes.

"Are you sleeping at all?"

My turn to shake my head.

She made a sound of distress and sympathy. "This is why
I don't want—can't let myself—get too involved with Trace.
It doesn't *work* with witches and mortals. This isn't your fault,
Cos. It was inevitable. Sooner or later we all find ourselves in
the position of either betraying our own kind or using magic

against someone we love. The best-case scenario is we spend our lives lying to them."

"It shouldn't have to be like that."

"But it *is*."

"But it *shouldn't* be. I should have been able to tell him the truth."

Andi looked alarmed. "Of course you couldn't. And you know why. Especially John, of all people."

I stared at her, wondering how she had learned of John's family history.

I didn't have to wonder long, though, because she said, "A cop? And not just a cop. A police commissioner."

"He wouldn't hurt me. Not like that." Whatever *that* was. I wasn't even sure. Were we talking about the bad old days of witch hunts and witch trials? Or the less bloody but equally devastating modern move of outing me on social media?

I insisted, "He wouldn't have posed a danger to any of us. He's not like that. He's angry because I lied to him, tricked him, tried to control him—and he's right to be. I-I vowed to put him before all others. But he's not vindictive, he's not vicious."

She looked sympathetic and not at all convinced. "I'm so sorry. It's all my fault. If I hadn't cast that cursed spell…"

"I don't know. If John and I were destined, then I'd have met him again anyway."

"But you weren't destined. You *aren't* destined. John is—was—just a-a circumbendibus. Your true beloved consort is still out there, still waiting."

I said nothing. She didn't mean to hurt me; she was trying to give comfort. In a minute she'd be telling me my best years were still ahead of me.

She must have read my face because she said softly, "And if I'm wrong, if you are destined, then it will work out."

I looked up quickly. "Yes."

We spoke of other things then, mostly work, before moving on to the topic of mutual friends. I told her Rex was still in a

coma and that Oliver had turned up unscathed. She told me that
V. and Bree were dating again.

"You're joking," I said. "Bree and V.? They tried that in
high school. It was a disaster."

Andi shrugged. "Maybe *they're* destined."

"Very funny. No way." A thought occurred to me. "Do you
think there's a chance Seamus was bi?"

"Seamus? No."

"Me neither."

"Why?"

"Those emails the police found on his computer, the ones
that led them to think he was having an affair, were from someone who signed themselves *V.*"

Andi gaped at me. She started to laugh. "And you think that
person might be *Vaughn*?"

"Well, no. Not really."

"I thought you were convinced it was the Garibaldi woman."

"It seems a lot more likely."

"I'll say!"

We were nearly finished with our meals when Andi said
slowly, hesitantly, "Has John ever talked to you about Somalia?"

"No." I studied her face. "I didn't know he— What about
it?"

"I don't know the full story, and Trace spoke to me in confidence. He wondered if John had told you."

I shook my head.

"It's just…something terrible happened there. Something
that changed them all—especially John—forever."

I said lightly, trying to hold back the tide of instant anxiety
generated by her words, "That sounds very dramatic."

Andi shrugged.

"You can't tell me more than that?"

Her hazel gaze flicked to mine. "No. It would be for John to tell you. It's just, I wonder… Trace said you're good for John." She smiled faintly. "He said you're an oddball, and not at all John's type, but you make him happy. That since he met you, John is more like his old self."

I felt a prickle behind my eyes, and stared down at my plate. "So much for that."

She said sadly, "I know you can't see it now, but maybe it's for the best. You did try so hard, Cos. And it seemed like you were having to do all the work, make all the concessions, make all the compromises. Maybe he's just not capable of feeling as deeply as you do."

Because of the terrible thing that happened in Somalia? Or because of another reason? Like the fact that he was descended from witch hunters.

I said, "I don't believe that."

But I can't deny that Andi's words shook me. I hadn't even known John had been in Somalia, let alone that something terrible happened there. I knew almost nothing of his life before me, and this was one more thing to add to the list—a list that was beginning to feel never-ending.

I said, "Thank you for telling me. I should probably get back to the shop."

"Me too."

It was her turn to buy, and after she paid, we stepped outside and said goodbye beneath the blue-and-white awning.

As she hugged me, Andi said earnestly, "Cos, everything will work out in the end. You'll see. Put your faith in the Goddess."

I hugged her back and nodded.

It wasn't that I didn't have faith in the Goddess. It's that I knew only too well, sometimes the Goddess answers no.

* * * * *

"Oh, there you are!" Blanche said brightly when I walked into Blue Moon a few minutes after leaving Andi.

Both she and Ambrose had such odd expressions, I glanced at the Orfac sun clock behind the counter. "Sorry. Am I late?"

"No, no." Blanche slid her gaze sideways.

I glanced at Ambrose, and he did the same thing: pointedly glanced sideways.

It's the kind of look hostages in films have when they want the police to know the mad bomber is right behind them.

I looked uncertainly to my right and saw that someone was indeed hovering. A tall man about my age with blond-streaked brown hair and smiling eyes.

"Surprise," Chris Huntingdon said.

"It is, yeah." I wasn't sure how I felt about it either.

He offered his hand, and we shook. His grip was warm and firm, not too aggressive, not like grasping a dead fish.

Blanche handed Ambrose a duster, gave him a little push, and they vanished into the forest of furniture on the other side of the showroom.

Chris was saying, "I remembered the night we met you mentioned owning an antiques shop, so I've been visiting antiques stores trying to find the right one."

"You're persistent, I've got to give you that." I guess I was sort of flattered, but I was also bewildered.

It must have showed, because he offered that appealing lopsided smile. "I know. You're probably thinking I'm some kind of weirdo stalker. I promise you, I'm not."

That's what all the weirdo stalkers say. But I smiled politely. "Okay. If you say so."

Chris winced. He threw a quick look in the direction Blanche and Ambrose had gone, and lowered his voice. "And it's not that I believe in love at first sight or anything like that. I'm not, you know, a *nut*."

I laughed. He laughed too, a little uncertainly.

"It's just that I felt a connection that night, and believe me, I know how ridiculous this sounds, not to mention inconvenient given that you're married, but I made a decision a few years

ago—don't worry, I'm not going to bore you with that story—
that I would never again let something good, maybe something
even potentially wonderful, slip through my fingers without at
least making an effort to see if it was real. If it could be real."

"That's…wow. I don't know what to say." Truth.

"I get it. Believe me. I know what you're thinking. Especially since your guy is a cop."

. "How do you know that?"

"You said. You said you were marrying a cop and your
family wasn't thrilled about it—which I have to say, did *kind* of
make you sound sort of sinister."

"Yeah, my father's a mob boss."

"You're kidding."

"Yes." I deadpanned, "It's actually my mother who's the
mob boss."

Chris laughed. He had a nice laugh. But I mean, who
doesn't? Laughter is a nice sound—unless it's unkind and directed at you.

He said, "And see, I'm still not scared off, so maybe there's
something here."

I shook my head, smiling but rueful. "That's nice of you,
but I really am crazy about my husband."

Crazy being the operative word.

"Aw." He grimaced. "That's sweet. Not what I want to
hear, but sweet." He tilted his head, considering me. "Did you
keep my card?"

"Nope."

"No second thoughts at all?" He studied me. His eyes were
brown. Not the fierce gold-brown of John's eyes. Chris's eyes
were softer, darker. The color of teddy bears and chocolate kisses.

I said, "None. Sorry."

He hesitated. "Can I buy you a farewell drink? Or a farewell cup of coffee?"

"No. Thank you, but I really do have a lot of work to get through this afternoon."

Chris sighed. "Well, at least I tried. Right?"

"Right."

He stuck his hand out again. "Okay, then. Goodbye forever, Cosmo."

We shook hands. "Goodbye, Chris."

He stared at our linked hands for a long moment, then turned away. He started toward the front door, then turned back. "I hope we're not making a mistake here. How would we know? What if you *are* the one? What if *I* am the one?"

I stared at him. Chris showing up here and now, posing that particular question was so *odd*. Like destiny with a capital *D* knocking at the door.

Except I already gave at the office.

I shook my head. "Timing is everything."

Chapter Thirteen

That night I opened the Drambuie we'd brought back from Scotland a million years ago.

I told myself I was trying out recipes for Andi's line of cocktail cupcakes, but truthfully, I just wanted to get plastered. And get plastered I did.

Also sick.

Very.

Drambuie is a proprietary liqueur the Scots have been making for about two hundred years. It's a blend of pot-still scotch and heather-flavored honey, and the taste is a bit dry, a bit aromatic. It's not really the kind of thing most people would choose to get drunk on. It would not ordinarily be my first choice, but the bottle reminded me of John. Reminded me of Scotland and our honeymoon. Reminded me that the last time I'd tasted Drambuie, it was on John's lips.

The classic Drambuie cocktails are the Rusty Nail and the Highland Margarita, but I was trying for something a bit sweeter and more delicate, so I opted for—in order of appearance—Autumn Leaves, the Kingston Club, and the Screaming Viking. I'm not sure why I thought a Screaming Viking would be sweet or delicate. Anyway, the two Kingston Clubs are what did me in, although the Screaming Viking didn't help.

The bed was spinning—and not in a magical way—when I finally collapsed. Unsurprisingly, I woke in misery a couple of times later. The third time I woke, the phone next to the bed was ringing, and Jinx was on the other end of the line, screaming and crying.

"What's wrong?" I dropped the receiver. Snatched it up again. "What's happened?" I was groggy as hell and feeling very unwell.

"Oh, Cos, get John," she sobbed. "He was *here*. He tried to *kill* me."

I stammered, "W-what? Who? Did you call the police?"

She shrieked, "John *is* the police!"

John. Right. The guy who didn't live here anymore.

I half fell out of bed, kicking free of the sheets, narrowly avoiding stepping on Pyewacket, who yowled in outrage and scooted under the four-poster. "Jinx, did you call 911?"

"Yes, yes. Can you guys come? Oh, Cos, can you guys hurry?"

I panted, "Yes, yes. We're on the way," still stumbling around in the dark, trying to find my jeans and shoes. My head was swimming, my heart thumping unpleasantly with the aftereffects of way too much alcohol as I dragged on my Levi's, shoved my feet into shoes, and yanked open the door to the 19th century wedding armoire. I pushed back the row of shirts scented of John's Eau Sauvage, climbed awkwardly into the cupboard, and croaked the words.

I arrived on the landing outside Jinx's apartment at the same time the cops did—which was about thirty seconds before John did. That meant Jinx's address was flagged in some mysterious way I knew nothing of, and it meant Dispatch must have known where to find John, knew that John was not currently residing at 1132 Greenwich Street. I didn't think of any of that until later. At the time, I was sick, shaking, and terrified.

The sight of John striding my way, looking sallow and stone-faced in the feeble overhead light of the landing, did not help my equilibrium.

"*What the hell are you doing here?*" he barked out.

The four—yes, four—uniformed officers jumped, thinking he was addressing them, then noticed me approaching from the left, and started to pull their weapons.

The apartment door flew open, and Jinx threw herself into my arms, sobbing. "Oh God, he was *here*, he was here in my apartment. Why would he come after *me*?"

"Who?" one of the officers asked.

I did a double take and saw that it was my old friend Officer Young. Young also did a double take and hastily holstered his weapon.

The other cops followed suit as Jinx cried, "The one on the news. The Witch Killer. He came for me."

"Spread out," John yelled. "Find that sonofabitch. He can't have gone far." He jabbed a finger at Young. "You're with me. I want to know how he got into that apartment."

I hugged Jinx tightly as the officers dispersed, weapons drawn once more, police-issue shoes pounding down the walkway. Suddenly she seemed so small and so young.

"Did he hurt you?" I demanded. "Are you sure you're okay?"

Jinx shook her head and then nodded. "I maced him."

If she was right, if it really had been him and not a garden-variety rapist, it was only thanks to the Lord and Lady that she was alive.

Doors were opening and then quickly closing again all down the landing. A few people in bathrobes and pajamas stepped out of their apartments, demanding to know what was going on. The officers ordered them back inside.

John took charge of Jinx, bumping me out of the way, pulling her into his arms. "Joan. Joanie, stop." He forced her to look at him. "We need your help. We have to know what happened. We have to hear the whole thing from the beginning."

She nodded, wiping her eyes.

He guided her into the apartment, where Officer Young was examining the front-door lock.

"I want a CS unit here now," John told him, leading Jinx to the sofa. Officer Young nodded and began to speak softly into his shoulder mic.

Jinx huddled on the green sofa, face in her hands. John said in a hard, flat voice, "You can go."

It took me a second to realize he was speaking to me. My head jerked up, and I stared at him. His eyes glittered like agates in his pale face.

Safe to say, time had not softened his feelings toward me.

I found I wasn't any too thrilled to see him either. I glared back.

Jinx half rose from the sofa. "What? Why? No, I want Cos here." She reached out to me, tugged at my hand, and I sort of folded onto the sofa beside her.

"I'm not going anywhere." That was largely bravado. I still felt wretched, and I thought there was a good chance John was about to have me tossed out of the apartment, but I wasn't going to willingly abandon her.

Besides, I needed to hear her story.

Jinx gave a wobbly laugh and pointed at my feet. "Cos, your shoes don't match."

I looked down. I was wearing a gray Vans on my left foot and a black loafer on my right foot.

"Jinx?" John prompted.

She nodded. Her face quivered, but she regained control. "After work, a bunch of us went out for drinks."

"On a Tuesday night?" John said disapprovingly.

I made a sound of disbelief. His frosty gaze met mine.

Jinx was focused on her recital. "Yes. And then when it got late, we went over to Maria's house—she's my friend from work—and we…visited some more."

John rolled his eyes.

"It was about two when I got home." She inhaled sharply, shakily.

I glanced around for a clock and saw that it was now just after three.

"Take your time," John said. "You're safe now." The gentleness in his voice closed my throat, reminded me of things I couldn't afford to think of then.

She nodded. "I-I thought when I walked in that it felt cold, like I had left a window open. I looked around, but no windows were open."

"Were the windows locked?" John asked.

She gulped. "I thought so, but the little jamb thing on the bedroom window sticks sometimes, so I can't always tell."

John's face grew grimmer. He looked at Young, who nodded and vanished into the bedroom.

Jinx said, "I undressed and went into the bathroom to take a shower. I turned on the water, and I was standing there brushing my teeth when I saw in the mirror that the door handle was… turning."

I put my arm around her.

She nestled against me, whispering, "I could see it turning back and forth, and I started to scream, and then I saw my purse was sitting on the toilet lid—"

"Why?" John asked.

"W-w-why?"

"Why was your purse in the bathroom?"

She looked confused. "Maria gave me some samples."

He looked more severe. "What kind of samples?"

I burst out, "What does it *matter*?"

His face tightened, but Jinx said, "Cosmetics. We have a new line of makeup at the store. I grabbed the mace out of my purse—"

I was expecting John to next point out the differences between pepper spray and mace, but he was silent, the lines of his face stark.

"The door burst open, and I sprayed him—"

"You saw him?" I asked quickly.

She shook her head. "He was just a blur. A dark blur. He was dressed in black. I started screaming, and then I heard him go out through the front. The front door banged shut, and I knew he was gone." She looked at me. "So I called 911, and then I called you guys."

Young stuck his head out of the bedroom and said, "This window doesn't lock, Commissioner."

John swore quietly.

I said, "Why do you think it was the Witch Killer?"

"Because…" She closed her eyes and shuddered.

"Because why, Joanie?" John prompted.

"Because of what he left on my bed."

John stared at her, stared at me, turned and went into the bedroom. Jinx raised her face to mine, her eyes huge in her white face.

"He found my athame, Cos. He left it lying on my bed. He was going to kill me like he killed the others…"

It seemed to take forever before the crime-scene unit arrived, although I know it can't have been long after Young called for them.

It also seemed to take hours before John finished talking to them, but at last he joined Jinx and me where we waited on the landing. He said to her, "All right. Let's get you over to Mother's."

Jinx had been drooping against the waist-high cement balcony, but she straightened up at that. "*Mother's?* Wait. I'm not going to Mother's. I'll stay with you guys."

John and I exchanged instinctive looks. John said, "Unfortunately, that's not going to work."

"Why? You have plenty of room. You have two guestrooms."

"She can stay at our house," I said.

"No, she can't," John said, giving me a long, level look. "She'll stay at Mother's." He looked at Jinx. "You'll be safest there. And Mother will love having you."

Jinx stared. "Safer than at your house? You have a state-of-the-art security system. You're the *police commissioner*."

John said wearily, "Joanie, will you just for once cooperate?"

"No, I won't. I'm not going to Mother's. I'd rather—" She gulped and said in a smaller, tighter voice, "If you don't want me, I'll call Maria. Hell, I'll get a hotel room."

"That's ridiculous. You're not going to a hotel. Think how Mother would feel if you didn't—"

Jinx burst out, "Mother can't stand me any more than I can stand her! I'll go to a hotel."

The officers and technicians still milling around the apartment landing exchanged uncomfortable looks. John thrust a hand through his hair, making it stand up in devil tufts. "Jesus Christ, Joan."

"How would you know? You were never there!" she cried. "She blames me for everything my father did. Every time she looks at me, she sees him!"

John looked stunned.

"She can stay at my old place," I said quickly. "I haven't rented it out yet. The bed's even still there."

John threw me an impatient look, but Jinx sagged in relief. "Yes! Okay, yes. I'll stay at Cos's townhouse. No one will know where I am. I'll feel safe there."

John muttered something, said brusquely, "Fine. Get whatever you need—check with the CS team first—and I'll drive you over."

The drive did not take long and was mostly silent. Jinx sat in the front seat. I sat in the back. Every now and then John's bleak gaze found mine in the rearview mirror.

I didn't know how to interpret that look. Safe to say, he was not delighted to find me in his company again. Maybe he thought I was somehow to blame for the attack on his sister.

When we got to Carson Street, I led the way upstairs. John, still silent, still disapproving, followed Jinx.

I opened the door, turned on the lights, and Jinx stepped inside.

Though it had only been a couple of weeks since I'd lived there, the rooms felt hollow and empty.

The last time I'd been here had been the night before John and I were married. John had come to me. He'd told me he didn't want to spend even a single night without me. The memory squeezed my heart.

I glanced at him, wondering if he remembered. He was looking at Jinx.

"Are you sure you want to stay here on your own?" he asked.

Jinx nodded stubbornly. "I like it. It has good energy."

He snorted. "Sure it does."

We said good night to Jinx and stepped out onto the landing, waiting for her to turn the lock behind us.

As I turned toward the stairs, John said, "I don't appreciate your second-guessing me in front of my sister."

"Yes, I saw that. I also saw that your sister was scared to death."

"She'd be a lot more scared if she knew whose—or what's—place she was spending the night in."

That got to me. I spun back to face him. "You're an ignorant, bigoted bully, John Joseph Galbraith. You don't know who or *what* I am because you didn't stick around long enough to fi —"

The problem was, I was still shaky, and that sudden move threw me off balance. I had a vertigo-inducing glimpse of the accordion of stairs stretching below me, and then John caught my arm, yanking me back, saving me from pitching down the stairs.

"*Watch it.*"

He instantly let go, as though I'd burned him. I reeled against the banister, truly shaken. A fall like that could kill someone. I pushed my hair back with an unsteady hand.

"Mistake. That would have solved all your problems," I said.

His eyes looked black, but as he watched me, his lip curled. "You smell like a brewery."

"I think you mean distillery. I drank your Drambuie."

"You're welcome to it." He was not being generous.

It occurred to me that I was fighting a losing battle. John could be way more unkind than I could. And without even trying.

I nodded and headed downstairs, gripping the railing as I went. John followed in silence. When we reached the pavement, he said, "I assume you can get wherever you need to go without my help."

For the first time, I wondered if I might get over John faster than I'd expected.

I said, "Yes. I can. But I think you should hear what I have to say, since it concerns the Witch Killer investigation."

He was not impressed. "Go on."

Not even an invitation to sit in his car. Which I would have appreciated because, June or not, it was chilly standing there without a shirt, in my mismatched shoes.

"You should find out if Ralph Grindlewood has an alibi for the night of the murders of Abigail Starshine and Clara Hellyer. You should also find out if he has an alibi for the night Rex was run down in that hit-and-run."

John's eyes narrowed. "You think your friend Grindlewood, the historian, tried to kill Rex? What would be his motive?"

"It turns out Ralph's not really a friend."

"Regardless, what would be his motive?"

"I don't know. Rex is still in a coma. But you're the one who told me Rex was a PI. Maybe Rex was working on a case involving Ralph."

"That's pure speculation. If not downright fantasy."

"Okay, but according to the eyewitness, Rex was deliberately run down by someone driving a black Mercedes Benz. Ralph drives a black Mercedes Benz."

"That's *it*? Grindlewood drives a black Mercedes Benz? That's what you wanted to tell me?"

"Of course that's not it. I-I can't tell you all of it. I can only—"

"*Déjà vu.*" He made a sound too bitter for a laugh. "Another French thing."

I winced at the memory of what had once been our private joke.

John's wolfish grin, his teasing, "I won't ask."

And my nervous, "It's a… a French thing."

It took discipline to let that go. I said, "I can tell you that Ralph isn't what he seems."

"Imagine that. Is Ralph a witch too?"

"No. No, Ralph is mortal. I thought he was an ally, a friend to the Craft. I was wrong. His interests and sympathies don't align with ours or with Wiccans. And that's the thing. Two of your victims were Wiccans, but the third—"

"There was no third victim."

"I know you don't want to hear this, but I'm certain—almost certain—that Seamus Reitherman was the third victim."

"You're right. I don't want to hear it. Because it's bullshit. I don't know what hold the Reitherman woman has over you, but—"

"Her *hold* is that she asked me for help. She knows that *I* know she's innocent."

"And you know that because…?"

"I told you this already. She wouldn't have tried to kill me if she hadn't believed I killed Seamus. It's obvious that her only motive for trying to shoot me was revenge for Seamus."

"It may be obvious to you, but it's not obvious to me or the detectives who worked the case, or Chief Morrisey, or the DA, or—"

"John, don't let your anger at me blind you to what's really going on. Don't take your anger at me out on Ciara."

"*Excuse me?*"

"I'm telling you there were…signs at the crime scene that indicated Seamus's killer was mortal."

"So, you're immortal?"

"No. I'm not immortal." My throat closed. I said huskily, "I can break my neck falling down a staircase like anyone else."

I could feel him trying to read my face in the gloom.

I said, "The term *mortal* is used to—that is, some use it to refer to the soul of the non-magic."

John's mouth curved into a sardonic smile. "I see."

And I was sure he did.

"So Reitherman's wife is not mortal. Naturally. Is *anyone* you know, besides me and my family, actually mortal?"

"Of course. Blanche is mortal."

Even though it was his suggestion, he looked taken aback. "That's *it*?"

"No. It's only that you're flustering me. I'm blanking on the others. Ralph is mortal."

"Yeah, right. Ralph. The bad guy. The one you think is behind this whole conspiracy to wipe out you and your coven."

"That's not what I said."

"Forget it. What signs were present at the Reitherman crime scene?"

I hesitated. "I can't really… You'll have to take my word for it."

John laughed. "Really? *Your* word?"

Anger was one thing. I expected his anger. I knew I deserved it. But his cynicism, his contempt, his instant challenging of everything I said or did… It wasn't right. *That* I didn't deserve. I hadn't lied about *everything*. Mostly I had *not* lied. I had acted in good faith in our marriage. To the best of my ability. I had tried—still wanted more than anything in the world—to make him happy.

I forced down my hurt. "John, I know you're—I know you hate me for what I did. But this isn't about us. Innocent people shouldn't have to pay the price because you don't trust me. You don't *have* to trust me. I'm telling you what I know—or at least what I think—and I'm giving you the names of those I believe you should look into. Can't you at least keep an open mind? What do you have to lose by investigating?"

He opened his mouth to tell me, no doubt in detail. I added quickly, "Why would I come to you with this information if I didn't believe it to be true? What do I have to gain by giving you more reasons to be angry with me?"

"How do I know what your plan is?"

I closed my eyes for a moment. "John. If you could just… remember these last weeks. Not as you view them now, but how they really were. Do I *seem* like someone with a plan? What would such a plan have been? What do you think you have that I need so badly, I would trap us both in…this?"

He was silent. Finally, he said, "Who else do you think we should be looking at?"

The fight drained out of me. What else was there left to say? "You should also check into the background of a woman named Valenti Garibaldi."

"Valenti?" John repeated slowly. "Isn't that Jinx's friend?"

"Yes. She's…" It wasn't only that telling these things to any mortal, even John, was difficult. To reveal such secrets to a police officer went against everything drummed into me since childhood. I felt like—I *was*—betraying a sacred trust. "She's involved in the Wiccan community. Both women who died were connected to her. And Seamus was—at least I think so—also connected to her."

He said, "Honest to God, if I didn't know what you were— if I hadn't witnessed it myself—I'd think you were crazy. You sound crazy. I'm not sure you're *not* crazy."

I said wearily, "I'm starting to wonder myself."

"All right," he said at last. "I'll see that Grindlewood and the Valenti woman are looked at."

"Thank you."

"Is that it? Are we done here?"

After a moment, I nodded.

Without another word, he turned, climbed into his Range Rover, and drove away.

Chapter Fourteen

June is a good time to visit Paris.

The days are long and sunny, the weather is warm but not too warm, the crowds are large, but not yet too large. The roses are in bloom, and it's almost impossible to walk down any street and not hear music. Or see a cat. Many, many of the cats of Paris are witches' Familiars. In fact, they say there are more feline Familiars in France than in any other country in the world.

Anyway, a small black Familiar had been following me since I left my hotel in Rue Jacob.

As much as I like Paris in June, I was not happy to be there. I was not happy about the reason for my trip, nor the trip itself. Eleven hours is a very long time to be stuck in a metal-and-glass container hurtling through the clouds. There are faster ways to travel than by plane, but it takes an incredible amount of energy and skill to cross an ocean. And the risk of accidentally entering a postern in an underwater sea cave or a shipwreck at the bottom of the sea is high. I don't know anyone who's actually tried it. Not me. Never me.

So I had landed Thursday afternoon, jet lagged and de-pressed, as well as edgy about my upcoming interview with the Société du Sortilège. I hoped a good meal, a strong drink, and a walk by the Seine would at least calm my thoughts, even if nothing could lift my mood.

And it was true—the fading afternoon sunlight on my face was pleasant, the smells and sounds of Paris comforting. Per-haps if John and I really were through—and it had certainly felt that way Tuesday night—I could move to Paris for a time. Blanche could run the shop without my help.

I walked slowly, lost in my thoughts along once familiar paths, passing houseboats and river cruises.

Of course, there was Ambrose to consider, but I couldn't help feeling that Ambrose's enthusiasm for being my apprentice was fading as fast as John's enthusiasm for being my husband.

That reminded me that I still needed to phone my mother. I got out my cell phone, and three tries later finally managed to reach her.

"Cosmo, *où étiez-vous*? I've been trying to reach you all day!"

"I'm in Paris."

I heard her small gasp. "*Ah.* He has filed for divorce." She barely bothered to conceal her satisfaction.

The pain was so sudden and unexpected, I put a hand to my chest. "No! He hasn't." Although I was sure it was only a matter of time. I wasn't going to admit that, though. "I'm here on the other matter."

"Is that true? Cosmo, I'm so pleased. You are demonstrating true leadership in your handling of this affair."

I made a gruff sound in my throat.

"Don't fear, *mon chou*. You will have to put up with a little scolding from withered old ones who don't remember what it feels to have blood running through their veins. Just bow your head and nod. The only one whose opinion matters is your Aunt Laure, and she is very fond of you."

"Maman, I wish to ask a favor."

"Of course, darling."

"Will you invite Joan, John's sister, to stay with you while I'm in Paris?"

After a pause, she said lightly, "*Très drôle, mon fils chéri.*"

"Yes, but I'm serious. I'm afraid she isn't safe on her own. I know she'll be safe with you."

"And what of the rest of us?"

I didn't bother to answer that. I'd have bet the house on *ma mère* versus any serial killer.

Maman said, "Why should I do this? I don't know this girl. *Je ne voulais pas ce mariage et je n'approuve pas la famille.*"

I said patiently, "*Je sais. Je demande une faveur à ma mère.* Regardless of what happens with John, I consider Jinx my sister."

I could hear the frown clear across the Atlantic. "What sense does that make? It is only through John that any tie exists."

"It's not only her safety I'm thinking of. Jinx claims to be a witch."

Maman made a pained sound.

"I know, but perhaps there is latent talent there. John—"

"That girl has as much Craft in her as a dumpling. You said John was descended from witch hunters on the paternal side. These two siblings do not share a father, *n'est-ce pas*?"

"Right. But even so. She's so sure. And there must be some reason the Society for Prevention of Magic in the Mortal Realm has targeted her."

"What makes you think they have? Cosmo, you leap to many conclusions. You cannot assume SPMMR is behind these murders. It seems most unlikely to me. Nor should you assume this so-called Witch Queen is working with them merely because she is *romantiquement impliquée avec* Grindlewood."

"Well, what *is* Valenti doing with him, then?"

Her chuckle was pure evil. "You're not that naive, *mon chou.*"

"No, I know *that.* I only mean, it's a lot of coincidences if she's not part of this SPMMR conspiracy."

"I'm not suggesting there is no connection, just that you are perhaps rushing to the first and obvious, not necessarily the most accurate."

I was silent, considering. Ralph had denied SPMMR's involvement, but he'd lie about that anyway. But given that SPM-MR knew Craft was quite distinct from Wicca, did it make sense to target Wiccans? Or was it their goal to wipe out every single instance of practice?

I said, "Either way, this would give you a chance to assess Jinx. You've never spent any real time with her before."

"For which I have been grateful."

"If she does have the potential, you'll know."

She sighed irritably. "And what will John have to say about this?"

"I don't know. I don't care."

She brightened. "I suppose he will loathe Joan's staying here?"

"I'm sure he will."

"*Bien.* The girl may stay here while you're away."

I smiled reluctantly, "*Merci, Maman.*"

I put my phone away and turned my attention once more to the green-gold swirl of water rushing along below me, eddying against the stone walls of the quay. I noted the dark watermarks from years of flooding, the giant rusted iron rings used to tie river barges to the docks, the odd iron grate or doorway leading to an underground passage, an ancient sewer system, metro portals, a yet undiscovered catacomb?

Like bedraggled homing pigeons, my dreary thoughts returned to Tuesday night's argument with John.

I cringed every time I thought of the things I'd said—the things he'd said. I was so horrible at trying to make my case. Maybe if I wrote it out? Maybe if I sent him a letter?

Or maybe not.

Eighteen-page missives—not even counting all the footnotes and addendums and tearstains—were always a mistake.

No. If I couldn't find a way to make John listen in person, giving him something he could ball up and toss in the trash was certainly not going to work.

Anything I tried was going to fail because John just didn't care en—

Something struck me hard between the shoulders. Like getting hit by a linebacker. I pitched forward, too astonished to even call out, lost my footing on the muddy grass, and felt myself falling.

I saw the glittering river glinting below—felt the shock of cold water rushing into my nose, mouth, ears as bubbles streamed past my terrified eyes. I sank into a bright yellow-green distance.

It takes longer to drown than you might think, and it is a terrifying process. I was flailing and kicking as I drifted down, but nothing seemed to be happening, and all the while I was instinctively—and what in the name of the Goddess is *that* instinct—gasping and gulping in water. I knew that was wrong, but I couldn't seem to coordinate the effort to stop.

I clawed desperately for the surface, yet I kept sinking, water burning in my nose, burning in my lungs, burning in my throat. I could hear myself coughing and choking, hear the sounds of panic and pain and the noise of bubbles streaming past.

The last time I nearly drowned, I had been a child, and I had blacked out so quickly, I really hadn't much memory of it. This agony seemed to go on and on and on.

Blackness edged my vision, I knew I was going to die, and I didn't want to. I wanted to live. I had a sudden, unexpected surge of energy, and I began to kick again. Hard. I shot up toward the sunlight, my head broke the surface, and I began to suck in huge, hurting lungfuls of air—which I coughed right back out again.

I was not alone. I was not miraculously swimming. Someone was towing me toward the shore in long, powerful strokes, and I dimly understood I'd had no sudden burst of energy. My oxygen-deprived brain had mistaken the efforts of my rescuer for my own actions.

I was still gulping and coughing and choking as we reached the muddy bank, where the waiting crowd dragged me out of the river and finally dropped me on the grass. All I could seem to do was wheeze and shake convulsively. Directions were shouted over my head. People—it seemed like a lot of people—began to pound my back and push my stomach.

When I could, I rolled onto my side and coughed up the dregs of the river onto the now pulverized and slimy grass. I drew a couple of sobbing breaths.

Hard hands fastened on my shoulders, dragging me upright.

I blinked dazedly into John's white, dripping face. His eyes were fierce, and there were harrowed lines carved around his nose and mouth.

He said harshly, "Are you all right? Cosmo? Can you get your breath?"

I wiped my eyes, nodded, gulped out, "I told you…a pool was…a terrible…idea…"

Chapter Fifteen

Nearly drowning in the Seine is not a quiet or private process.

The police came. The firemen came. The news reporters came. Every tourist in Paris came—with their cell-phone cameras held high.

There was a lot of activity and a lot of questions.

No, I had not seen who pushed me in.

No, I had not noticed anyone following me. (I hadn't even noticed John following me, which was proof of how lost in my own concerns I'd been.)

No, I could not think of anyone who wished me harm.

Fortunately—depending on how you looked at it—John had witnessed my being shoved into the river, so at least there was no suspicion that I'd tried to kill myself or was emotionally unstable and trying to get attention. There were several theories as to my mishap. Perhaps it had been a robbery gone wrong. Perhaps it had been a prank gone wrong. Perhaps I had attracted the attention of someone emotionally unstable and trying to get attention.

The whole situation was embarrassing and awkward, but it gave me time to absorb the fact that John was really there. Not a hallucination of my oxygen-starved brain. He had followed me to Paris.

He had saved my life.

When the police car dropped me off at my hotel, John came along too. I didn't know why, but I was grateful.

Somehow, the hotel management had been alerted to my misadventure, and we were informed there were extra blankets and a hot water bottle waiting in my room. They offered to launder and press John's now dry but wrinkled and stained clothes, but John declined. He was not staying, he said.

I had expected that, but it still hurt to hear. He did go upstairs with me and wait for room service to bring up a pot of hot tea on a tray. John declined the tea. I drank two cups, but was still shivering when I jumped into the steaming shower.

The tea and the scalding shower helped a lot to clear the mists, and by the time I stepped out of the bathroom, warmly wrapped in my navy bathrobe, I had recovered my wits enough to wonder what exactly John was doing in Paris.

I had half-expected him to be gone, but he was standing at the one of the tall windows overlooking the hotel's small courtyard. Only John could look that tough and imposing in river-wrinkled clothes.

"Would you like to use the shower?" I asked.

He glanced at me. "No. But I could use a drink. Does the hotel have a bar?"

"Yes. It does. And I'm more than happy to buy you a drink, but why are you here, John? How did you know I was in Paris?"

"Bergamasco."

Cryptic, even for John. I said slowly, "You mean Sergeant Bergamasco was following me?"

"Correct."

I sat on one of the brown velvet overstuffed club chairs. "But why?"

John said curtly, "Just be glad he was."

I stared at him. I was glad not to be dead, of course, but I was not thrilled at the idea that John trusted me so little, he had assigned Bergamasco to tail me.

"Thank you for saving my life. I sincerely hope you don't get gastroenteritis for your trouble. But why was Sergeant Bergamasco following me? And why did you follow me to Paris?"

He said calmly, "I want to know what you're up to."

I tried to answer with equal calm. It wasn't easy. "I came because I need help. And SFPD hasn't been much so far."

He didn't like that, but all he said was, "But you can get help here in Paris?"

There was still so much he didn't know—and probably didn't want to know. So much I couldn't tell him even if he had still cared for me.

"I hope so. I have family here."

"Oh yes," he said dryly. "Your family. And all those *French* traditions."

I held his scornful gaze with my own. "You didn't believe that anyway."

"No, I didn't. But I sure as hell didn't suspect the truth."

No, of course not. No one expects the…well, the truth.

I said instead, "You could have sent Bergamasco. You didn't have to come yourself."

"Fortunately for you, I came myself."

He was still not answering the question. That was interesting.

"You could have just asked me."

He said sardonically, "And you'd have told me the truth?"

"I'd have tried to be as truthful as the situation permitted. I didn't like lying to you. I never wanted to."

"Not good enough."

All at once I'd had it. I stood.

"Really, John? You really think honesty is always the best policy? You think the world is a safe and accepting place for people like me? We lie for our safety. We lie for our survival. Which you should now understand, given that your sister nearly died only a couple of days ago simply because someone *imagines* she's a witch. It could be Andi next. It could be me. It nearly *was* me today."

I don't think I'd ever known him not to have an answer, but that was just was well. I wasn't done yet. "You're right. I was wrong to marry you if I couldn't be honest. I know that now. I should have called off the wedding the minute I knew the truth. I was weak. I'm sorry. I will regret that mistake all my life. All I can do now is try to make it right." I had to stop to steady my voice. "I promise you I won't contest anything in the divorce. Take what you like. Take it all. I don't care. None of that matters to me."

He didn't speak. Didn't move. Was it maybe a little disappointing to prepare for war only to find you'd already won?

Now came the hardest part. "*But.* I'm not going to apologize for what I am." Humiliatingly, my voice shook. "You made it clear on Tuesday night that you think…what you think. So mote it be. We—all of us—are as the Goddess made us."

He moved restively, started to speak, but then folded his lips together and looked out the window.

So that was that.

I wanted to believe he had followed me because he still loved me, because he wanted me back. But getting me back didn't require a plane ticket. He had to know he only had to say the word.

Even as this thought formulated, something in me rebelled. More. Recoiled.

No.

The last few days had changed me. At this point, it would take more than John telling me he forgave me to convince me there was any sense in returning to our marriage.

Oh, I still loved him. I probably always would. And I still took full responsibility for my actions. I'd meant what I said. I knew it had been wrong to proceed with the marriage once I discovered his love for me was probably still partly based on enchantment.

Not that I hadn't given him plenty of opportunity (and incentive) to pull out. I had allowed myself to be convinced there was no harm, no foul by John's pragmatic, hell, even cold-blooded reasoning for moving ahead. But ultimately the blame was mine because I'd had all the facts. John had not.

I had relied on not being able to tell John the full story as an excuse not to be honest with him. But that was a false equation. Having determined I could not tell John the truth, it behooved me to break off our relationship. I could have come up with any number of excuses, or none. It would have hurt him, it would have been expensive and awkward and embarrassing, and he might have ended up as angry and hurt as he was now, hating me as he did now, —but it was still the right course.

Too late, I saw it clearly.

I also saw that by entering into a relationship under false pretenses, I had ceded all power to John. Ours had never truly been a relationship of equals. Knowing what I did, fearing that his love was not strong enough to withstand much pressure, I'd backed away from trying to assert myself, from being honest, from being *me*. And honesty being the foundation of intimacy, how strong had the bonds been between us?

As it turned out, not strong at all.

So, the idea of going back to that? Returning to status quo? Not as appealing as I would have once believed.

Busy with my own epiphany, I was startled when John said finally, tersely, "I came for the reasons you stated. You could be next. And it looks like you were right because that guy shoved you. It wasn't an accident."

"Again, *merci*. Thank you for jumping in after me. I appreciate the gesture. I should have taken you up on those swimming lessons."

His face went bleaker still. Well, and I can't deny I was taking a masochistic pleasure in rubbing salt into both our wounds.

John said, "What's your plan? Do you have one?"

"Yes. Unfortunately, I can't really discuss it with you. But yes. Also—"

"Also?" John prompted at my sudden stop.

I cleared my throat. "Also, I must inform my—the head of my family that my marriage is…over."

Just for an instant, there was something in his eyes. Some turbulent mélange of emotions: confusion and hurt and anger. Something like I felt. Like I had been feeling since he walked out of our marriage.

In the next instant, it was gone. Maybe I had imagined it.

"I see. Where does this leave us?" He hastily corrected, "After you speak with whoever you're going to meet, what happens? Is there some kind of witch police force?"

"Uh…no."

"Then how does this work?"

"Well, I mean, I'll ask for advice and get council—"

His expression was almost comical. "That's *it*?"

"No. Of course not. Not entirely." I tried to explain. "It doesn't— It's not like—"

"Is the person who killed those women, the person who came after Jinx, the same person who came after you?"

"I don't know. I'm assuming yes. I'm not sure."

"Is this person a witch? Do they have magical powers?"

"Again, I'm not sure. I don't think so. I think this person is mortal. I'm almost sure."

"So you really don't know anything. And there is really no practical help to be had from whoever it is you're here to see?"

"Not practical in the way you define practical."

John gave a disbelieving laugh. "Okay, give me your definition of practical."

"Once I have a better idea of what I'm dealing with, I'll—hopefully—be able to come up with a plan for stopping them."

"Him. The person who pushed you into the Seine was male."

"Did you get a good look at this person?"

"No. He was wearing jeans and a white hoodie with skull and crossbones on the back. I didn't even realize he was also following you until he pushed you in."

"He may not be working alone."

"Great." John was silent, thinking. He said abruptly, "Let's get a drink."

We drank wine in the pretty little courtyard that opened from the downstairs lounge.

White and green umbrellas leaned over white iron tables and chairs with green cushions. Comfortable, but not so comfortable that you'd want to spend more than an hour or so. Ivy spilled from urn-shaped planters. Purple and pink petunias were planted between the slate flagstones. The tranquil *plish-plash* from the fountain at the far end ensured all conversations remained private.

There were two other couples in the garden. An older couple, smiling and comfortable with each other after a day of sightseeing, and a pair of newlyweds gazing soulfully into each other's eyes, whispering things to make each other blush.

They made me a little sad because I knew now that John's and my story was coming to an end. In fact, having suggested we go for a drink, John seemed to have nothing to say to me. But eventually the wine, the golden light through the trees, the warmth of the cobblestones—the simple pleasure of being alive on a beautiful day—lulled me into a sense of peace.

It was as I'd said to John upstairs. *So mote it be.*

We finished our first round, and John got us a second.

I took the glass, saying, "I shouldn't have this. I haven't eaten more than a handful of Cheez-Its since Andi and I had lunch on Tuesday."

John gave me an unreadable look.

We sipped in silence. The shadows lengthened. The newlyweds went upstairs. The older couple left for dinner.

John said idly, "So are there also werewolves and vampires?"

"Where?" Comprehension dawned. "*Oh.* Not—that is, I met a vampire when I was a child. She was very, very old even then, and she's crossed since. I've never met another one. I suppose they've either died out or are very rare. And I've never known *anyone* who came across a werewolf, or a were-anything."

"What about wizards?"

I hesitated. "Wizards are different. It's an entirely different magical tradition. Craft is almost universally based on bloodline and generally evolves in matriarchal societies. Wizardry is typically a masculine occupation, and it's not…genetic."

He nodded thoughtfully.

I said, "Also, though it's mostly academic now, wizardry was originally commercial in intent."

"Witches are born. Wizards are made."

I nervously cleared my throat. "Generally speaking."

"Ghosts?"

"Ghosts are real, yes. Of course."

He said, "Of course." Silence. Then he said, "What about elves, fairies, trolls? Fairytale stuff?"

I gave a shaky laugh. It was such a crazy conversation to have—and with John, of all people. He threw me a quick, scowling look, which instantly sobered me.

"Maybe once? I don't…I don't have any experience with such beings. I think they existed in historical times. In fact, I'm quite sure they existed in historical times. Now I assume—believe—they're extinct. Like dinosaurs and dodo birds."

He nodded absently. "What about Martians?"

"I-I'm sorry?"

"Extraterrestrials. Other life forms."

"I don't— How would I know?"

He said harshly, "I have no idea what you do or don't know. Everything I understood about life on this planet has been turned on its head. Suddenly witches exist and magic is real. Why not space aliens?"

"John," I began helplessly. But I didn't know what to say. Of course this was a shock for him. Maybe more of a shock for him than someone else because he was so...earthbound. He had renounced the very idea of a god—was not just unaware; had consciously rejected the concept. I had found no sign of spirituality in his life. If he couldn't see it or it wasn't backed by science, he didn't believe in it.

I said instead, "I don't know about life on other planets. I assume there *is* life on other planets. It's hard to believe we'd be the only sentient beings in a universe so vast, we can barely conceive of it. What I do know is on this planet there are some things you have to take on faith."

He shook his head, denying this.

I said tentatively, "Have you told anyone about...what you now know? Have you told anyone about me?"

"No."

I relaxed a fraction. This had been the thought that most terrified me, for both our sakes.

I was less comforted when he said, "No one would believe me."

"Maybe they would. You're not someone to make up stories."

He grunted in agreement.

When we finished our second glass of wine, he said, "I should go."

I had never previously considered that one of the most painful phrases in the English language, but it was. It was excruciating.

I said calmly, "Yes. Of course."

He rose. "Will you be all right?"

I nodded. "Yes. I'll be fine."

Hungry though I was, I thought I would probably sleep until midnight when the Société du Sortilège convened.

He hesitated. "Maybe I'll see you to your room."

I grinned. "How gallant. But I think I'll be safe walking through the hotel lobby."

"You're still my husband. It's my responsibility to make sure you get in okay."

I was a little amused, but maybe a little moved. He did still care for me. He hadn't hesitated even an instant about jumping into the Seine to pull me out. Although he probably would do that for anyone.

We left the cooling temperature of the garden and walked upstairs, where it was still warm. When we reached my room, I unlocked the door, and then turned back to John.

I said softly, "I just want to say again, thank you. And I'm sorry. Truly sorry." I felt I had to clarify. "Not for being. I was born this way and won't apologize for that any more than I apologize for being gay. But I'm sorry I wasn't honest. I know you won't understand, but I *couldn't* tell you the truth. I don't have the right. It's not my secret to share. But that being the case, I shouldn't have married you. It was wrong. I wronged you."

"You said that before," he said crisply. "Guess what? That part I *do* understand. Classified information. Need to Know. I didn't have security clearance." He shrugged. "But like you say, that being the case—and given that my feelings for you were not based on reality—you had no fucking business going ahead with our marriage."

I hung my head. "I know," I whispered.

John suddenly groaned from deep in his chest, said roughly, "So *why* do I still want you so much?"

I glanced up in surprise as his hand locked on the back of my head, tangling in my hair, pulling me to him. His warm mouth claimed mine.

For a paralyzed moment I could think of nothing but the feel of John's hard, insistent lips on my own, the almost feverish heat, the taste, the scent, the shocking urgency of John's need.

He pushed the door open, and we half fell inside, still clutching each other, still kissing. We made it to the bed, falling onto the creamy comforter on the cloudlike mattress.

"Why you, why did it have to be you?" he muttered, breaking contact for a moment. His eyes glittered, and I could see his resentment, his reluctance, but I could see longing. Knew it because I felt it too.

I shook my head, gasped out, "*Le cœur a ses raisons que la raison ne connaît point.*"

He leaned forward again, his hot mouth bruising mine, but he relented almost at once. I recognized my name in the soft, persuasive pressure of his mouth. *Cosmo.*

Not a question. A call. A summoning I had no strength to resist.

The terrible, exultant familiarity of it. A reminder that I was not even close to being over John, that no matter how fast I ran or how far I traveled, any distance between us was all on John's side. Reason and logic could not withstand the power he had over me—still had—whether I wanted it—whether *he* wanted it. Incurable yearning sparked, then blazed back into life, a dying star crackling at the edge of the buckling universe.

It *had* to mean something that he was here. No spell had brought him to me. He was real. He was now. And he wanted me too. The sudden unbearable sweetness of it made my breath catch and tears burn beneath my lashes. I was parched for him, withering without him, and there was no remedy for this drought, no cure but John.

I cried out in shock when he pushed me back.

"Are you doing this to me?" John's voice was ragged, his chest rising and falling, his pupils dilated so his eyes looked black as midnight.

"W-what?"

"Is this a spell? Are you making this happen?"

"*No,*" I protested. "This isn't— I'm not—"

"Then where did these feelings come from?"

Anger, frustration, hurt soared. I planted my hands in his chest, shoving him back so hard, he nearly fell off the bed.

"Where do you think they come from? This is *lust*, you bastard. Nothing more, nothing less. And it's all you. It's not me. I don't want you. I *hate* you."

I shoved him again, but this time John didn't budge. Didn't speak. His big hands locked on mine like iron bands, holding me in place. He stared at me unblinking, unmoved.

"*I hate you,*" I repeated fiercely, and yet even I could hear the lack of conviction. "You left *me*, remember? So leave me alone. Haven't you done enough? You've ruined my life."

A sob tore from my chest.

Yes, I know, according to the *Malleus Maleficarum*, witch-es can't cry because the tears of the humble can penetrate heaven and conquer the unconquerable, so tears are an offense to Satan, blah, blah, blah. Of course we fucking *cry*.

Another sob—painful, ugly—ripped out of me at the lack of comprehension on his face.

"Cos."

I didn't hear the rest of it. Maybe there was no rest of it. To my eternal humiliation, I was weeping openly. I tried to pull away, but his hands tightened, and instead of releasing me, he drew me to him. His shoulder was painfully familiar because once I had found comfort there, comfort in his arms. I could smell the earthy, woodsy scent of his aftershave, feel the warmth of his skin beneath the cotton of his shirt, hear his heart beating against my own.

"All I did was fall in love with you," I gulped into his neck. "How is this fair? Even when I found out you were descended from witch hunters, I *still* loved you. And what do I get? You *destroyed* me…"

What a world, what a world. Who would have thought that you could destroy my beautiful wickedness?

I mean, I don't pretend it was anything but childish and undignified.

"Okay, stop." John's deep voice resonated in his chest, and that made me cry harder because it reminded me of when we'd talk late at night and... Oh, it doesn't matter. Because it was all over, and I was just making it worse by carrying on.

After another moment or two, John said more gently, "Jesus. Come on, Cos," and ran his hand over my head. "Shhh."

I don't think he meant to. I think old habits die hard. The strands of my hair crackled against his fingers—static electricity, not witchcraft—and his hand lingered just a bit, grew caressing, and then stilled.

"*Shhh*," he said again, and I quieted.

We sat like that for a little while. I knew he would pull away soon, but I couldn't make myself pull back first. Also, it's amazing how exhausting it is to cry like that.

Finally, John said, "I'm not trying to hurt you."

"No. But you're very good at it." I pulled back, and that time he let me go. I could still feel the indent of his fingers on my wrists. I wiped my face, not looking at him.

"I can't trust you. I can't trust anything I feel for you. Never again."

I did look at him then, and I could see... I wasn't sure what that expression meant. I think there was regret, but there was resolve too.

I wiped fiercely at my still wet cheeks. "Same here. But let me reassure you about one thing. I'm not *making* you want me. I can't *make* you do anything. Magic doesn't work on you."

His eyes narrowed. "That's a lie. You told me Andi—"

"Yes, she did. And the spell did work. For a time. I'm now sure it would have faded quickly even if I hadn't made her remove it."

His lip curled.

"You remember the day of our wedding rehearsal, don't you?"

"Of course I remember," he said impatiently.

"You remember when that piano fell out of the townhouse next to ours and nearly killed me?"

His brows drew together. "Yes. You know I do."

"That's my point. You shouldn't. You shouldn't remember anything about it. That spell I tried to use on you was a forgetting spell. It should have wiped the memory from your consciousness. It worked for a few seconds, but then you started to remember."

John stared at me. Although we had briefly covered this ground the night of the party, I don't think he had fully absorbed the implications—and I hadn't been about to point them out to him when he was mad enough to kill me.

"That should be impossible, yet somehow you were able to throw off some of the effects of the spell. Then later that night, when I tried again. In fact, I tried twice that time."

His mouth curved in self-mockery. "When I thought you were trying to hypnotize me."

"Right. I tried again to use a forgetting spell, and it didn't work. You were immune to it. The more I tried, the stronger your resistance grew."

I could see that this time, the significance of my confession was not escaping him. And I knew by drawing this connection for him, I was giving him an advantage he didn't need. The advantage was already his.

"Honestly, the fact that your first impulse was to rationalize what had happened should have warned me something strange was going on."

"Should have warned *you* something strange was going on?"

"Yes. You should have been freaking out, John. You should have been afraid. *I* was. I was trying to use *magic*, and you were coming up with all kinds of reasonable explanations for what was happening. Hypnosis? *Seriously?*"

He opened his mouth. Closed it.

"It's like something in your subconscious allowed you to process what happened and put it in an acceptable context."

He frowned, remembering, considering.

"There's more," I said. "To me, this is the clincher. When Ciara interrupted the wedding ceremony at our house—" I stumbled a little at the bleakness in his eyes.

"Yes?" His tone was curt.

"Ciara used a holding spell, a spell that kept everyone present—except you—motionless."

At his apparent lack of comprehension, I said, "There were other witches present besides me, but the only person able to act, able to stop Ciara, was *you*."

I could see this thought had never occurred to him. "I don't believe you ever even realized magic was used. I think you acted out of age-old instinct."

"How would that be possible?"

"I don't know. Something in your bloodline, I suppose. Some kind of built-in immunity."

He was silent. When he finally spoke, he surprised me by changing the subject. "What about Jinx? Is she a witch?"

I temporized. "What if she is? Is it going to change the way you feel about her?"

"Of course not. She's my kid sister."

He seemed sincere. In fact, he seemed almost affronted at the very idea.

"I don't think she is. But I can't be sure. I'm out of practice."

"What does that mean? You're out of practice."

"Just that. I don't—try not to—use Craft. Like any skill, like any muscle, it weakens if you don't exercise it."

"It's only been a few weeks."

"No. I stopped using Craft almost two years ago." He started to speak, and I corrected, "At least, I made the decision. I'm not saying I always stuck to it."

"Clearly not. You used it to get to Jinx's apartment the other night. You used it—"

I said irritably, wiping my wrist against my wet eyes, "I *know*. That's what I'm trying to say. As a matter of fact, I've used it more since I met you than in the last two years."

He ignored that. "Why did you renounce your magic?"

"It didn't have anything to do with you, and I didn't renounce it. Not formally. I just wanted to live an ordinary life. A normal life. Mortal life seems so simple, so uncomplicated. I wanted that for myself."

He seemed struck by this, frowning at me in a grim sort of silence as he worked through whatever it was crowding the airwaves.

"What about now?" he asked finally.

"What *about* now?"

"Are you going to continue with your…Craft, or are you going to try to live a normal life?"

"Does it matter?"

He hesitated, then gave a quick, brief shake of his head. "No. I guess not."

It wasn't that I'd hoped… Well, yes, I probably *had* hoped even without admitting it to myself. But anyway, so much for that.

I said, "Is there anything else? Is the third degree over? Because I've had a *horrendous* day so far, and I could use some sleep."

John nodded curtly, and rose. He stood over me for a moment.

I gazed into his eyes. Neither of us spoke.

John sat down again.

I don't know who reached out first.

Chapter Sixteen

Our clothes whisked away as if by magic.

It wasn't magic, though, it was desperate desire that had us tearing off jeans and shaking off shirts before landing back in each other's arms. My nerves were humming a sexual incantation as John's hands moved over me with easy familiarity, caressing and stroking, and I climbed onto my knees, wrapping my arms around his shoulders. My cock jutted up, moisture pearling at the tip, and his wand tapped mine.

"Feels like a fucking lifetime," he groaned.

I nodded. It did. It felt like forever. I kept my jaw locked on all the foolish, emotional things I wanted to say—the wonder of being in his arms again, of feeling his mouth pressed to mine, of being permitted to touch and taste what I had believed forever lost. Was perhaps still forever lost. For John, this was just sex. For me…better to think about it later.

He nuzzled me beneath the ear, his mouth trailing burning kisses down the length of my throat. I moaned, letting my head fall back.

"*Oui?*" John muttered.

I laughed breathlessly, "*Mais oui. Certainement.*"

He continued on, lingering only to lick and kiss before his mouth returned to my own. His tongue thrust into mine, and I pushed hungrily back, sucked. French kiss.

This was one thing that had not changed. Our own personal, private magic. We could still set each other alight with just a touch, just a kiss. It had been there from the first night. An instant, instinctive sexual compatibility that enabled each of us to answer the unspoken wish in the other's heart.

I ran my fingers through his hair, those short silky strands the color of fire, pressed my face to his throat and licked him, licked at the little pulse beating above his collarbone.

John groaned, "I swore I wasn't going to do this…"

I ignored that, nuzzled him, and his mouth latched on to mine. His kiss deepened. I let myself sink back into the downy nest of pillows and comforter, and he lowered himself onto me, warm and solid. I liked his weight on me, liked the roughness of his jaw against my own, liked his taste and scent and the feel of his fingers against my cheek—and the insistent prod of his cock in my belly.

Our naked bodies rubbed against each other, starting to find that rhythm, my own cock rock hard and requiring attention, jutting up, nestling against his.

A sultry, snapping energy started at the base of my spine, tingling and sparkling up through cartilage, blood vessels, and nerves.

"*Ne t'arrête pas*," I pleaded. "*Ne t'arrête pas*." Not that I really thought he would stop. He was as lost in the moment as me.

One final jerk, one final thrust, and climax came tumbling like a shower of stars falling from heaven, glittering hot release.

John was still thrusting against me, and I gathered my dazed wits, arching my back, trying to give him the force and friction required.

"Uh…uh…uh…" Choky little animal noises tore from my throat.

He surged against me, spilling out all the heat and hunger and heartache of the past few days.

Another couple of tight jerks, and he collapsed on top of me, breathing harshly.

I closed my arms around his wide back, closed my eyes, waiting—braced—for whatever came next. I thought he would resent giving into this and was liable to say something hurtful. Or maybe he would say nothing, just get up and go.

He didn't speak, though, only shook his head once as if in disbelief, and lowered his head to the curve of my shoulder. I closed my eyes.

I woke stiff, sticky, and despite the fact that I was wrapped in John's arms, chilled. The room was dark, and through the half-open window I could see stars in the blue-black sky.

I didn't move. Didn't want to wake John, but he was already awake. He said, "I should go."

I said nothing.

I could feel his erection prodding my belly. Tit for tat. My own cock was stirring, pointing in accusation.

He said, "I didn't dislike you."

I turned my head. "What?"

He said quietly, "The night before the wedding, you said I disliked you when we first met. I didn't dislike you. I thought you looked like a guy who had never been told no. It put my back up. But I didn't dislike you."

That was probably true. It's one of the rules about casting love spells. True love cannot be kindled where it can't survive.

Granted, it was unlikely John's feelings for me had ever been true love.

But the point is, it takes more than a love spell to change hate to love. Or hate to infatuation.

I said, "Thank you for telling me."

We lay there for another minute or two, and then John sat up. He winced and felt his back. "Jesus. I'm getting old."

I closed my eyes. I didn't want to watch him walk away again.

He stood up, said, "Lift up. Let's get under the blankets."

It was lovely, the two of us cocooned together in that comfortable gloom, and I squirmed pleasurably, surrendering to the finger stroking that delicate pucker of skin and muscle.

"Oh *Goddess*. Touch me again there…"

"Where? Here?" John whispered.

My breath hitched, words temporarily failing me. I pushed my hips down, trying to get more. And more he gave me.

I writhed, breathless, helpless, shivering with a kind of electrical overload at the feel of that long, sturdy finger probing me, pushing in and out past the guardian ring of muscle.

"How's that?"

I nodded. John's lightly haired legs brushed my own, his breath hot against the back of my neck, his arm resting warmly, possessively over my waist as he began that delicate caress of fingertip to anus once more, trailing up and down the cleft of my ass. My breath caught.

"Okay?"

"Yes." Stupid to get emotional, but I'd thought this forever lost, something relegated to dreams, or a memory to comfort myself with on winter nights.

John kissed my shoulder. One finger became two, and then he replaced the fingers with his cock, pushing slowly, with piercing sweetness, into my body. A tight fit, a very tight fit. John was taking great pains not to ram into me, which I appreciated, my body instinctively bracing, resisting…

"Oh Goddess. Yes. Please, John."

An earthly act that somehow crossed into another realm. So much more than physical.

I'd have liked to lie on my back, liked to have the lights on so I could stare up into John's face as he made those huffs of anguished pleasure, liked to have seen John's cock sliding in and out of my body, the better to remember him by, the better to remember every treasured moment of this night by, but it was safer this way, easier on my pride for sure that John not see my face, not know how much it meant.

Almost at once we began to move, at first off-kilter, but then finding the meter, sliding into it, gliding into the push… pull.

We were fucking hard now, losing the last inhibitions, letting go. The sheet gusted over us like an inquisitive ghost. John was thrusting fiercely, satisfyingly, and I was shoving back to meet him. We urged each other on with groans and inarticulate words over the excited squeak of the bedsprings.

"Does the bed speak English?" John muttered, and I laughed. It was such an unJohn comment, but then I hadn't known him long enough to know.

John's hand smoothed over my flank, found my cock, and worked me with that deliberate skill. I moaned and frantically rocked my hips.

"*John...*"

John's thrusts punctuated his words. "I miss you so...fucking...much..."

Heat and pressure built with an almost unbearable pleasure until it seemed that something *had* to give...and then it did. I stiffened head-to-toe as release crashed through, sweeping me dizzily along. I began to come in great, glittery gushes, only dimly aware when John grabbed me, losing his own rhythm, losing control at last and crying out as he toppled off the edge after me...

S̲oft greenish light, like sunlight, filtered through spring's first unfurled leaves... My eyelids flickered, lifted. I raised my head.

A pair of green eyes blinked at me from the bottom of the four-poster. A cat was softly purring.

The little black cat of the afternoon. The calling card of the Société du Sortilège.

Sur mon chemin, I thought.

The cat's mouth opened in a soundless *meow*.

John slept on, silent and motionless as a monolith—and just as inscrutable—his arm wrapped possessively around my waist.

I denied myself the pleasure of a final kiss—I couldn't risk waking him—and eased out from under his hold. I slid out of the bed and began to dress hurriedly.

When I was ready, I soundlessly inched open the door. The cat slipped through, and I followed her out into the gloomy chill of the hallway. I finessed the door closed and waved my hand before the lock. I whispered, "*Sweet deep sleep, my love shall keep.*"

The spell was unlikely to work on John but would hopefully keep anyone else from disturbing him.

I turned and followed my guide down the stairs, through the shadowy lobby, out the twin doors of wood and glass.

The night air was cool, scented with the smells of damp flowers and old stone. If possible, Paris by night is even more beautiful and intoxicating than Paris by day. And once the stars come up, the crooked alleyways and shrouded side streets of St. Germain are a little quieter, a little more magical than other parts of the city. Though I heard laughter or the occasional melody drift from open doorways, I saw no one as I followed my silent guide.

The Familiar trotted down another narrow street, and I strode after her. Once I heard a *scritch*, and spun around. The pavement was empty.

Or was it?

About half a block down, I thought I saw motion in the shadows of a lamppost.

The back of my neck prickled. Was someone really there, or were my eyes playing tricks on me?

The cat meowed. I turned and saw her standing half in and half out of a postern beneath the awning of the back entrance of a closed bookstore.

I raised my hands, spoke the words, and followed her through.

I stumbled out into a large antechamber deep underground. A small torch illuminated a room lined floor-to-ceiling with skulls and bones.

Yes, for reasons I have never understood, the Société du Sortilège convenes in a secret chamber of the Empire of Death, also known as the Catacombs of Paris. Two hundred miles of ossuaries running five stories below the City of Lights. The bones of six million Parisians lie in a labyrinth of tunnels so long and complicated, there are large unmapped—even undiscovered—sections (and that's without the benefit of obfuscation spells).

It's a little creepy, no denying, but as places of power go, the Catacombs can't be topped. Some of the oldest skeletons date back to the Merovingian era, more than 1,200 years ago.

I shivered. The tunnels are always chilly, and the scent… the scent is hard to describe: something reminiscent of dusty incense, moldy churches, and mushrooms. I glanced around for my guide, but she was gone. That was all right. I knew where I was. The waiting room to The Sorcerer's Chamber.

A ghostly voice whispered, "*Cosmo Aurelius Saville, Duc des Westlands…*"

I stiffened my spine and entered the adjoining chamber, which was larger and brightly lit by four braziers. A portrait of my aunt Laure in her youth hung on one wall.

Three men and four women sat at a long curving table. Two of the members were new to me, but I recognized my Great-great-aunt Oreguen, Countess of Rennes, and my cousin Gilbert, Viscount of Eyskens, as well as Lord Snowvale, Head Librarian Gertrude Smith, and Oliver Sandhurst.

I did a double take at the sight of Oliver. He didn't bat an eye.

There are always 137 active members of the Society, but only seven top-ranking members sit upon *le Conseil Savant*. Their number does not include the Crone or (occasionally) the Hermit. In fact, the council's original purpose was merely to advise and assist the queen or king. But over time they have become a kind of governing body.

"Your Grace," Madame de Darrieux began as I knelt before the council. "You have requested this emergency convening of the Société du Sortilège. What is it that brings you before us?"

She spoke in French, of course. The whole meeting took place in French, but to make things easier, I'll just give you the rundown in English.

I rose and explained that I was there on behalf of Ciara, who, as the lawful consort of Seamus Reitherman, a witch of the Abracadantès tradition, was entitled to claim protection from the Society. And I gave my reasons for believing Ciara was innocent of the charges filed against her and why I felt the Society should come to Ciara's aid.

My cousin Gilbert said, "Pierre Sjoberg is handling her case, isn't he? He's the best there is when it comes to navigating the mortal judicial system." He glanced at Madame de Darrieux. "The Society can pick up her legal expenses, I imagine?"

Madame de Darrieux nodded graciously. "I think we can all agree to that."

"I'm sure she'll be very grateful, but I think she's hoping—I'm hoping—that we can do something more."

"Such as?" Gertrude Smith inquired crisply.

"Such as finding out who actually murdered Seamus."

"He was murdered by a jealous lover," Gilbert said. "We all know that." The others nodded, glancing at each other.

"But that's just it. I don't think he was. I think he may have been killed by an agent of the Society for Prevention of Magic in the Mortal Realm. And I think it's possible his death is tied into the murders of several local Wiccans."

I expected them to be shocked by this news, but they seemed only politely interested.

"Why should you think so?" Madame de Darrieux inquired curiously.

I proceeded to detail why I thought so, and I'll be the first to admit that I probably didn't explain as well as I could have.

I didn't have much to go on—fewer facts than feelings—but I suppose I'm used to having my feelings taken more seriously.

"It seems very unlikely, old boy," Gilbert said at the end of my narrative. His smile was kind, his tone avuncular. Gilbert's only ten years older than me, but he acts like it's forty.

"SPMMR is nonviolent," Madame de Darrieux said.

"But I thought—"

She cut in. "Yes, there has been the occasional punch-up—is that how you say it? A few bloody noses, the odd concussion, a broken arm in Rome. No one has *died*. The idea that one of their members would stab Seamus to death…why?"

"For the *Grimorium Primus*."

"But he had sent the *Grimorium Primus* to you, no? So that makes no sense."

"They obviously didn't know he'd already sent the *Grimorium Primus* to me."

She shook her head. "No. No, this seems quite impossible. There must be another explanation."

"Okay, but then that's my point. Shouldn't we—the Society—discover what that explanation might be?"

They exchanged startled looks, which then grew amused or indulgent, depending on the face.

"Dear child, we are not detectives. We are not investigators," my Great-great-aunt Oreguen protested in her tiny creaky voice.

"No, those of us in this room aren't, but we do have detectives and investigators within our tradition. We could surely call upon—"

Madame de Darrieux said briskly, "Your Grace, your compassion becomes you, but these are mortal matters. You've said yourself that Seamus's death seems to be tied into that of these Wiccans; therefore, it follows that he had involved himself in the affairs of mortals—and paid the price. This is not a matter for the Société du Sortilège."

"But these women are *dying*."

"And that is a tragedy. But it is a mortal tragedy. We cannot involve ourselves in the affairs of mortals."

"You say that as though it were one of the Ten Precepts, but it's not. It's not a-a *thing*. Wiccans are…they're our sisters and brothers."

That did not go over well.

Even Gertrude Smith, who had been listening intently through my exchange with Madam Chairman, looked startled at my assertion.

Madame de Darrieux took a moment before saying, "Your Grace, your divided loyalties are understandable, and as the son of the heiress to *trône de sorcière*, your wishes are of importance to all of us, but we cannot accommodate you in this matter. There is nothing more to be said."

Gertrude Smith spoke up. "Unless there's another matter you wish to address?"

I couldn't believe what I was hearing. But it was clear from their expressions that I was not going to win them over. The matter was closed.

It was tempting to walk away then and there, but just because they were not, in my opinion, fulfilling their duties did not excuse me from fulfilling mine.

"There is one other matter."

"Yes?" Madame de Darrieux prodded.

"My… It seems my marriage is…may be coming to a close."

This got a reaction. It was as though a wind swept through the chamber, stirring papers, sending hats flying—even though there were no hats or papers present. The relief in the room was palpable.

"You are divorcing the mortal John Galbraith? The marriage is over?"

I tried to speak steadily, ignoring the pain it gave to say the words, "It seems so."

"*Well!*" Madame de Darrieux's eyes were shining. "This is unexpected news."

"Praise be to the Goddess," Great-great-aunt Oreguen exclaimed. "How I have prayed for this."

I said nothing. In fact, for a second or two, words would only have been embarrassing.

"Thank you for bringing this to our attention," Madame de Darrieux said. "You have the sympathies of us all."

Yeah, sure.

But I nodded.

"That's not the extent of it," Oliver exclaimed. "You must tell all of it. The mortal knows you're a witch!"

"*What?* Is this true?" Madame de Darrieux was on her feet.

I ignored her, staring at Oliver. He too was on his feet, pointing at me, as though he was in a Vincent Price film, denouncing me to a tribunal. His eyes seemed to glow with a fanatical light.

What. The. Heck?

How could Oliver possibly know that?

"How is this possible?" Madame de Darrieux demanded.

"It's true," I admitted. "He found out…through a series of unfortunate events."

"You told him!" Oliver cried.

"*Did* you tell him?" Gilbert questioned.

"That was one of the unfortunate events, yes."

That was not the end of it, I assure you. And even after I had promised them multiple times that John posed no threat to anyone in the Craft, they were unconvinced and seething.

No threats were put into words, but by the time I left the Catacombs, the sun was up and the church bells were chiming. I could not help but wonder uneasily for whom those bells tolled

Chapter Seventeen

John was not in my hotel room when I returned from my meeting with the Société du Sortilège.

There was no note, no sign he had ever been there, and though I wasn't surprised, it did sadden me. I wasn't so foolish that I imagined the fact we'd had sex meant our problems were over, but I had hoped there might be a little softening on his part.

I caught the first flight I could, and landed back home at 6:55 Saturday morning. I went straight to my mother's.

I arrived outside the dining-room doors just in time for breakfast. Unlike me, my mother is an early riser. But breakfast was not being served in the mansion on Nob Hill. From the sounds issuing through the solid oak doors, it seemed that vitriol with a side of jealousy was on the menu.

"I'm not a poodle," Phelon shouted. "I'm not going to sit around here day after day waiting—hoping—you might deign to drop in!"

"So long as I am paying your kennel fees that is exactly what you will do," Maman shouted back.

I winced. There is a reason Maman, unlike her twin sister, Countess Iolanthe Saville Whitby, did not enter the French Ministry for Europe and Foreign Affairs.

"Maybe I don't need you to continue paying my kennel fees," Phelon cried. "Or any other fees. Maybe I'll be paying my own fees from now on. And how is it this spa of yours doesn't have a phone? Maybe *I* should be the one looking at credit-card statements."

I heard the sound of breaking glass. Maman shrieked. I threw open the door to the dining room and saw Maman picking up the remaining half of a pair of black Chinese cloisonné vases decorated with yellow celestial dragons. The other vase lay in pieces around Phelon, who was cowering in the corner behind the dining table.

"That's an antique!" I protested.

Maman jumped. "Cosmo, will you never learn to knock?"

"I was knocking!"

"Knock louder," Maman snapped. She set down the cloisonné vase. "Get up, Phelon. You look like the poodle you claim not to be."

Phelon jumped to his feet. "That's it! I've had enough. I won't stay under this roof a minute longer."

"Then you had better pack quickly," *ma mère* retorted.

Phelon kicked aside one of the fallen dining table chairs and strode from the room.

"*Bah!*" my mother exclaimed. She glowered at the tall doors through which Phelon had vanished.

I said, "I hate to interrupt breakfast, but I wanted to check on Jinx."

"You'll have to do it at her mother's home."

"I don't understand."

"John dragged her out of here at the crack of dawn."

This was confusing, not least because I'd sort of thought *this* was the crack of dawn.

"But why? What did he say?"

"He said he was more than capable of protecting his own sister. He said he did not approve of my influence on an impressionable girl." She tossed her head. "Good riddance to both of them."

No, clearly he had not softened at all.

"I'm sorry, Maman. I hoped— It doesn't matter. Was she very difficult?"

Maman made a little moue. "*Non*. She was no real trouble. In fact, she's rather amusing."

I hid my smile. "Is she a witch?"

She shook her head. "I could find no sign that she possesses Craft."

I expelled a breath. "Okay. I guess I'm not surprised."

My mother made a noise of exasperation. "But there *is* something there. I sense…something. She is not a witch. Not yet anyway. But…"

"But?"

"But she is not *not* a witch."

I stared. "What does that mean?"

"I have no idea. I would have liked to spend more time with her. It pains me to say this, but I believe she should receive training."

My own feelings were mixed. It was a relief to know my instinct about Jinx had been correct. But this news would not make John happy, and it would only further complicate his relationship with his sister.

"You're not alone. Valenti Garibaldi seems to think so as well."

"Mm…" Maman scowled. "There must be something in their dam's bloodline. I can't imagine what." She gave a delicate shudder. "*La femme est un troll*."

"Not literally, I hope."

She said dryly, "So do I."

"Did Jinx leave willingly?"

"She wasn't happy, but she didn't refuse to go with him, or of course I would have interceded on her behalf."

The thought of that intercession made my blood run cold.

Maman tilted her head, regarding me. "What did you gain by your audience with *le Conseil*?"

"Nothing. They have no interest in Seamus's murder or the murders of these women. They'll pick up Ciara's legal fees."

"That will be no small thing."

"Ciara was hoping for more. So was I."

"You're an idealist, Cosmo. You get that from your father. This is not a world for idealists."

I don't think I *am* particularly idealistic, but I didn't argue the point. I have ideals, of course, but one reason I thought I could make my marriage to John work was because I know ideals are often unrealistic.

"Did you speak to your aunt?"

"No. She wasn't there. There was a Madame de Darrieux running things."

Suddenly I had my mother's full attention. "Thérèse de Darrieux?"

"I don't know her first name. She was about your age."

"Dark eyes, dark hair, aquiline features?"

"Her hair is platinum, but otherwise, yes."

"Ah-ha." My mother scowled into space. "So. Thérèse has resurfaced at last."

"Who *is* Thérèse?"

"She's a distant cousin. Ambitious, ruthless…"

Yep, clearly a blood relation.

My mother shrugged. "*Eh bien.* I got rid of her once. I'll get rid of her again. But this does complicate matters."

"Does it? Which matters?"

She patted my cheek. "Nothing to trouble you, *mon chou.* Thérèse has always wished to take my place in the line of ascension. Nothing new there. I know all her little tricks. It is discomfiting that she has wormed her way onto *le Conseil*, but in her place, I would attempt to do the same."

None of this was very reassuring, but if life with Maman has taught me anything, it is that sometimes ignorance truly is bliss.

"There were several new members on the council, including Oliver Sandhurst."

"Oliver?" Maman's elegant brows arched. "*ça me surprend.*"

I asked guardedly, "It surprises me, but why does it surprise you?"

"Oliver's standing in *la Société* has been shaky for many years. Some of his attitudes and opinions are irregular, even for an academic."

"That's what I thought. I couldn't remember the details. It was something to do with his books, right? He didn't have all the permissions required?"

"A little more serious than that. He revealed information never intended for mortal eyes regarding the Craft, particularly of the Abracadantès."

"It seems all is forgiven."

Her smile was odd. "And yet ours is not a forgiving tradition."

No, ours was not. Which meant what exactly?

Had I got it backward?

I had jumped to the conclusion that Oliver was being menaced by the Society for Prevention of Magic in the Mortal Realm. What if it was the other way around?

What if Oliver was working for our enemies?

What if Oliver was a double agent?

And if that was the case, who within the Société du Sortilège was working with him?

* * * * *

After I left Maman's house on Nob Hill, I took a chance and popped into City Hall.

I do mean popped in. I entered through a postern on the third floor and took the elevator up to the commissioner's office. Pat's desk was empty, but John's door was partially open.

I could hear the restless shuffle of papers and Ella Fitzgerald crooning "They Can't Take That Away from Me."

I poked my head in and found him sitting at his desk, reading over a file.

I knocked on the doorframe. John's head jerked up, he stared, and a quick succession of emotions played across his face: surprise, pleasure, suspicion…and then nothing. He regarded me impassively.

"I hate to bother you," I said.

His mouth twitched, but straightened. "Since when?"

"I thought you'd like to know what I found out at my meeting."

He pointed at one of the two chairs in front of his desk.

I left the doorway, sat down.

He held up his mug. "Coffee?"

I shook my head. "You made good time getting home."

"So did you."

I started to speak but, in my haste, swallowed wrong and started to cough. John rose, came around the desk. I caught my breath. Shook my head.

"Sorry. I swallowed a speck of fairy dust." John drew back doubtfully, and I smiled. "*Totally* kidding. It was just a normal, ordinary dust mote."

He shook his head, his expression derisive, though whether at me or himself was unclear. He leaned his hip against the corner of his desk and picked up the file he had been reading.

"Your father sent me your astrology chart."

"Oh," I said uneasily. "Did he?"

"He did. I thought he was an astronomer?"

"He is. He does, um, take an interest in astrology. But I mean, that's natural."

"Is it?" John gazed down at the paper he held. "He believes I should be aware that you are 'gentle, affectionate, curious, adaptable, and possess the ability to learn quickly and exchange ideas.'"

I cleared my throat, said, "Nothing you didn't know."

"Nothing I didn't know," John agreed. "He says that you are also 'nervous, inconsistent, and indecisive,' and I should be prepared to be patient."

I felt myself turning red. "That's not very fair. I don't think I'm inconsistent."

John didn't reply, continuing to read from the report. "'There is much childish innocence in the nature of this Gemini. He recognizes love first through communication and verbal connection, and finds it as important as physical contact. Not surprising, then, that Cosmo has spent a lot of time with different lovers, waiting to find the right one who is able to match his intellect and energy. He needs excitement, variety, and passion, and having found that right person, the lover and friend combined into one, he will be faithful and determined to always treasure—'"

"You can stop now," I said. Loudly.

John grinned. For a moment he looked like his old self. The self I fell in love with. The self I believed did really love me.

I said, "You should see what he wrote about you."

"I bet."

For a moment or two we just gazed at each other, smiling.

Belatedly, I recalled my mission. "So the people I went to see in Paris? It was no-go."

"No-go?"

"They aren't going to be any help in solving these murders."

"I see." He corrected, "Or no, I don't. But at least, I can say I'm not surprised."

"I am. And disappointed. But that's the situation. These crimes will have to be solved by SFPD without outside help."

"That's usually how we do it," he said gravely.

Yeah, well, he still didn't know what he was dealing with. But then, in all honesty, neither did I. Not really. And after the reaction of the Société du Sortilège, I was afraid to say anything more. Afraid for John's sake above all else.

I changed the subject. "Is Jinx—"

At the same moment, John said abruptly, "Anyway—"

He stopped, nodded for me to continue.

I said, "Maman says Jinx is staying with your mother now?"

"No. Jinx has made it clear that she would rather be burned at the stake."

An unfortunate choice of words.

He added, "She went to stay with her friend Valenti."

My spirits sank. "Did she?"

"Is there some reason she shouldn't?"

I shook my head.

"You don't look convinced."

I said, "For reasons I can't explain, I wish Jinx wasn't so tied in with her."

After a moment, he admitted, "I think anything I say will make the situation worse."

"I think you're right." I considered. "I'll try to talk to her. Hopefully, *I* won't make it worse."

"She does seem to think a lot of you."

"Puzzling, isn't it?"

He smiled faintly.

Time to go. It was so hard, though. It was always going to be hard.

I gathered my nerve. "Paris was nice."

He nodded. "It was."

"Not the nearly drowning part, of course, but later." *Why, oh why couldn't I shut up?* Like he didn't know I didn't mean the nearly drowning part?

It wasn't easy, but I made myself ask, "Is that going to be it for us? Was that the last time?"

"Cos…" No question John was in pain too. Knowing should have helped, but it didn't.

"Okay. I just…needed to know." I tried to smile, but it was a dismal effort. "No point asking if the answer is always going to be no."

He sucked in a sudden breath and looked away. A muscle jerked in his cheek.

I didn't know what else to do, so I stood up. "Right. Well, I guess there are things that will have to be worked out. I'll… wait to hear from you."

He nodded, his face expressionless, his eyes watchful.

I hesitated, but what on earth was I waiting for? I went out, closing the door softly behind me.

Chapter Eighteen

It took me several hours to find where Valenti Garibaldi lived. Eventually, I had to resort to a finding spell, and even that took time, which was in itself revealing.

It was evening when I reached the green and white Queen Ann Tower Victorian on Fulton Street.

I rang the doorbell. A minute later Valenti opened the door. She wore a red velvet tea gown embroidered with tiny blue and yellow and purple birds.

"Merry meet, Valenti."

For once I saw her unguarded reaction—she was utterly flabbergasted.

"Cosmo. What in the— What are— How did you find me?"

I hadn't been wrong, then; she had been using an obfuscation spell. Old-school but generally effective. Except that I was a bit old-school myself.

I smiled. "I let my fingers do the walking."

Zero comprehension. She was still struggling with the fact that I'd managed to break through her spell.

I said, "Is Jinx staying here? John said that was the plan."

"Uh, yes. Joan is here. She's staying for a few days."

"Would it be all right if I spoke to her?"

She hesitated, which raised a few alarm bells for me, but then she got hold of herself, smiled, and opened the door.

"Of course. Won't you come in."

I followed her down a short hall into a U-shaped living room with a small marble fireplace. The house was lovely, one of the quintessential old Victorians: large light-filled rooms, dramatically tall windows and ceilings, a gorgeous grand staircase, and beautiful white woodwork.

She invited me to sit, and I chose a chair near the fireplace with its photo-crowded mantel. "I have to say, Cosmo, you're much more adept than I realized."

"Really?"

"Yes." She gave a self-conscious laugh. "I'm embarrassed to admit I thought you were all sparkle and no spell."

"Ouch."

"Well, it's just the way you present yourself. You seem so…frivolous, so inconsequential. And then, of course, you married a mortal. It was hard to take you seriously."

I murmured, "Was it?"

"Would you like some peppermint tea? I was just brewing a pot."

Tea is tricky. Sometimes a cup of tea is just a cup of tea. Sometimes it's something else. I wasn't sure I was willing to ingest anything Valenti brewed until I knew her a lot better.

"Thank you, no."

She permitted herself a small smile, as though she knew exactly what I was thinking.

"I'll go and see if Jinx is available."

The moment she left the room, I jumped up and went to study the photos on the fireplace mantel. I wasn't sure what I was looking for. Some hint as to who she was before she became the Witch Queen? A hint as to where she came from? Anyway, they were the usual thing. The gap-toothed kindergarten shot, the first pony ride shot, summers at the lake shots, family holiday shots, the high-school grad shot, the college grad sh—

I turned back to study the family holiday photos. Mom, Dad, Valenti, and a kid who was vaguely familiar but did not look much like Valenti.

I peered more closely.

Who the hell was that kid? Why did I think I knew him?

I moved from the fireplace to check out more framed photos on the white built-in bookshelves. Absently, I noted a small library of books on philosophy, metaphysics, and the occult, but my real interest was the family photo gallery.

There he was again. A tall, gawky kid with shaggy brown hair and a lopsided smile.

My heart stopped.

Chris.

Valenti said from right behind me, "I'm sorry, Jinx isn't feeling well. She said she'll call you tomorrow."

I barely registered it.

I pointed to a photo of her and Chris taken at what appeared to be a Halloween party. They looked young and drunk and happy. Both were dressed like witches. "Is this— Who is this?"

A shadow crossed her face. "Chris. My brother."

"Your brother?"

Her green gaze grew curious. "Stepbrother. If it matters."

"But he's not... He's mortal, isn't he?"

She looked wary. "Do you know Chris?"

"Yes. That is, we've met."

"When did you meet?" Yes, she was definitely wary—but also puzzled.

"At a dance club. Misdirections." I clarified, "It was before I married John. We danced a few times."

Something in her expression sent a feeling of unease crawling down my spine.

"You danced with him?" she asked, and now she was doing her best to give nothing away. "He was here? In San Francisco?"

"Yes." And now I was the one trying to give nothing away. "He was nice. Charming."

"He is charming," she agreed automatically.

"And he's mortal."

After a moment, she nodded. "Yes. He's mortal."

"How does that work? Does he know about you? About the Craft?"

"Yes," she answered reluctantly.

I could see there was more—a lot more she wasn't telling me. I could see that every moment we spoke, her worry was mounting. No. More. She was frightened. She was putting two and two together and making a connection I had not yet drawn…and it was frightening her.

"*How* does he know about the Craft?"

She considered not answering, but then seemed to give up. "Both parents were witches."

"But… How can that be? Both parents witches and he's mortal?"

"Yes."

"But that's not possible." Actually, I had no idea whether it was possible or not. I'd never heard of it before.

"Clearly it is." Her expression twisted. "Believe me, it's possible. Had there been *any* trace of magic in him, it would have been found. There was nothing he wanted more. Nothing any of us wanted more for him."

"Was he tested?"

She said impatiently, "Of course!"

We eyed each other, neither speaking for a moment or two.

She said carefully, casually, "By any chance, do you know how to reach him?"

I shook my head. "He gave me his card, but I didn't keep it."

She let out a soft breath. "I see."

I said, equally careful, equally casual, "Does he have friends here in San Francisco?"

"I don't know. I haven't spoken to him in two years. We… fell out."

"Over the Craft?"

"No. Yes." She shook her hair back restlessly. "Yes and no. When we were growing up, everything was fine. He—we all—believed his powers would manifest with time. They never did, and he grew bitter about his lack of…ability. But then a few years ago we joined the Society for Prevention of Magic in the Mortal Realm." Her green gaze met mine.

"Yes. I'm confused as to how that works with being a practicing witch."

"You know as much as you need to for now." She was still following her own troubled thoughts. "SPMMR gave Chris focus and purpose, but gradually he became so…aggressive in his approach. We disagreed more and more as to how the Craft should be policed." Genuine pain glistened in her eyes. "Eventually, we stopped speaking."

"Aggressive?" I questioned.

She added with a hint of her own aggression, "He's not alone in feeling that way."

"Aggressive like…violent?"

"Of course not!" She was not terribly convincing.

"There's more here than you're telling me."

"Because it's none of your business."

"Valenti, if what we suspect is true—"

"No," she said quickly, fiercely. "There is no we. This will be handled within the organization. If there's anything to handle. I don't believe there is. This is… Anyway, you're wrong. It *isn't* true."

I was following my own thoughts, slowly working it out. "But it makes sense. An outsider who isn't really an outsider. Someone who knows the inner workings of the Craft. Someone who could perhaps fake his way—"

"You need to go."

"That's how he chose Jinx. You're the connection," I said. "*You* connect all the victims, including Seamus. He's been following *you*."

"Get out."

"It isn't just everyone around you. He could turn on you too. He probably will. If he thinks he's on a mission—"

"*Get out!*"

"My leaving doesn't change—"

She raised her hand, and the row of tall windows flew open, lifts banging against the sash locks. A sudden wind whipped around the room, billowing the curtains, buffeting me, pushing me toward the hallway.

I let it scoot me across the polished floor and down the hallway.

I stumbled out the front entrance. The door slammed shut behind me.

John's cell phone rang and rang and then went to message.

I was pretty sure he wasn't blocking me. For one thing, I was calling from our house number, so he'd have been blocking his own number, and for another, I felt certain that after Paris he would take my calls, even if he didn't want to be married to me anymore.

It was worrying because in the four—now five—weeks I'd known him, he never turned his phone off.

I was stumped for a minute or two, and then I remembered that old standby, the phone directory.

There was a good chance the number might not be listed, but no, there it was: *Bergamasco, P.* followed by the correct street address.

I dialed the number, and after a couple of rings, the sergeant's deep voice said, "Bergamasco."

"Hi, Sergeant. Is my—John there?"

He hesitated.

"I think he'll talk to me, but you can tell him it's police business. It's related to the Witch Killer case."

Bergamasco sighed. Heavily. "He's in the shower."

"Okay. Well."

"I'll tell him you called," Bergamasco said.

"Thank you."

Dial tone.

Chapter Nineteen

Fifteen minutes later, John phoned back.

"That was a long shower," I said. "There's a drought going on, you know."

He was all business. "Pete said you have something urgent relating to police business to discuss."

"I have a lead on who the killer might be."

Far from being excited, his tone was resigned. "What kind of lead? Where did this lead come from?" I didn't have to be able to read minds to know he believed I was coming up with excuses to phone.

My face burned, but I said briskly, "It's a guy named Chris Huntingdon. He's Valenti Garibaldi's stepbrother, which is why, even though I don't have the kind of proof or evidence or whatever it is you would need, you have to take a look at him. I'm worried about Jinx."

"I'm worried about Jinx too," John said, "but I can't start rounding up citizens on your say-so alone. You're going to have to give me more."

"Okay, well, here's the problem. I'm not a detective, and I don't know how to get you what you would need. I'm telling you this so that you can order the right people to find the evidence."

John said impatiently, "It doesn't work like that."

"Well, this time it has to. The connection between all these cases, including Seamus's murder, is Valenti. She's the V. in his emails. I don't know if they were actually having an affair or not, but something was going on between them. Enough that Seamus came to Chris's attention."

"All right, look," John said in a tone that brooked no argument. "I've already asked Chief Morrisey to have Iff and Kolchak take a second look at the Reitherman case—which did not go over well, for the record, but which is being done. So, if that's what this is about, you already got what you wanted." He added grimly, "And you may have put yourself back in the crosshairs achieving it."

"If you'll—not you personally, obviously—but if your detectives will focus on Chris, I won't have to worry about that because Chris is the killer. I know it. I can't prove it, but I *know* it."

He was silent for a moment. Then he said very quietly, "Is this a witch thing?"

"*Yes.* Which is why I can't give you much more than I already have. I shouldn't even be talking to you, John. That's the truth."

"Why shouldn't you be talking to me?"

"It's… It doesn't matter, really. If you could just focus on Valenti as the nexus of these crimes, I'm confident you'll find the evidence you need. But it would be better for everyone if you didn't drag your feet."

To my relief, he didn't argue. Granted, he didn't agree. But at least he seemed to be thinking it over.

"And also, I think you should get Jinx out of Valenti's house as soon as possible."

"I'd like nothing more, but I can't force her."

"You don't have to *force* her. You could try persuading her. For starters, why don't you tell her what's really going on with us, so she understands it's not that you don't want her staying here. I mean, if we're getting divorced, we can't hide it for much longer anyway." Thankfully, my voice stayed steady and calm even on the word *divorce*. Maybe I was finally coming to terms with the situation.

"Why shouldn't you be talking to me?" John asked again. I could hear the frown in his voice. "Are you in some kind of trouble?"

I said lightly, "Nothing a good divorce lawyer can't fix." It didn't sound light, though. It sounded bitter.

John didn't say anything.

"Sorry," I said. "I don't want to do this. I don't want to talk about us. I just want you to please, *please* listen to what I'm saying and find Chris. Find him before he hurts anyone else."

"Do you have any idea where to find him?"

"No. He gave me his card, but I threw it away. I've looked for it, but the trash has been emptied since then."

John said slowly, carefully, "He gave you his card?"

I expelled a long breath. This was the part I had really not wanted to get into. Not now anyway. "Yes. I met him at Misdirections the night of my stag party. We danced, he wanted my number, I didn't give it to him. But I ran into him—"

I stopped, remembering that Valenti had still been sitting in the bar when Jinx and I had bumped into Chris at Spruce. Had Valenti been lying about not seeing him for a couple of years? She'd seemed to be telling the truth. Either way, whether Chris had been following her or meeting her, I felt this confirmed my conviction that he was Seamus's murderer.

"But you ran into him?" John prompted.

"At lunch with Valenti last Friday." It seemed like a million years ago. "He gave me his card and asked me to call if I ever wanted to grab a coffee or something. I threw the card away."

"I see. You don't remember anything from the card? Area code? Was it a PO Box?"

"Sorry. I really don't remember anything about it." I cleared my throat. "I should maybe mention he also showed up at Blue Moon."

"*What?*"

"He was still pushing for coffee. He seemed to feel there was some connection between us." A chill ran down my spine. "At the time I thought he was sincere. Now…"

"Does he know you're a witch?"

"Given what I know now, it seems highly probable."

"Fan-fucking-tastic." John said crisply, "Okay, I'll make sure there's a black and white parked outside the house. You're not to open the door to anyone who isn't a cop or you don't know personally. Got it?"

I said uncomfortably, "I don't think that's necessary."

He wasn't listening. "And I'll get Jinx out of the Valenti woman's place if I have to carry her out myself."

"And that's definitely not a good plan."

But I was talking to myself. John had already hung up.

"You'd have liked that little Familiar in Paris," I was telling Pyewacket as I undressed for bed.

Pye flicked an ear, watching through slitted eyes as I went over to the window and peered down.

As John had promised, a black and white police car was parked right in front of the house. The car had an official gleam in the moonlight. A pretty good deterrent to any potential evil-doer, I'd say. I wasn't worried, in any case, because I knew there was a very sturdy obfuscation spell on the house, courtesy of my father. Not enough to fool a witch, but we weren't dealing with a witch.

I glanced back at Pye. "There's something about French Familiars. *Very* sexy."

He opened his mouth in a silent laugh, showing all his white, wickedly sharp teeth.

"I think we'd be happy in Paris. Remember how much we liked Domrémy? Anyway, it would just be for a year or so. Just to get a little…emotional distance."

…

"True, but it's probably safer for John, if you think about it. If I'm not around, I'm clearly not divulging additional sensitive information. Really, there's a good chance he'd forget all about—"

Meow.

"Okay, well, maybe not. But there's a good chance *they'll* forget about him."

…

"Anyway, I think it's for the best. The move, I mean. I can't stay here, and I don't feel like I can fit back into my old life. I think a fresh start, a change of scenery, is exactly what we need."

…

"Right? My thoughts exactly."

I climbed into bed, turned off the lamp. The shadow of Pye crossed through the bars of moonlight and curled on the pillow behind me. I settled my head more comfortably.

I'd spent the hours after my conversation with John trying to use a finding spell to locate Chris, but despite my best efforts, I hadn't been able to come up with any clue to his whereabouts. He remained an uncomfortable blank whenever I tried to reach out toward him.

Anyway, I'd done what I could. The rest was up to John and SFPD.

It felt like weeks since I'd really slept, but I didn't think all the worry and heartache in the world could keep me awake tonight.

I closed my eyes. Pye placed one velvety paw on my forehead and began to lick my hair…

S-*s-s-s-s-s-s-s…*

A snake-like hiss next to my ear.

I jerked awake, opened my eyes to darkness and the tiny warning *squeak* of the doors of the 19th century wedding armoire.

I knew instantly what had to be happening, but my mind rejected it as impossible. Because even when you believe in magic, some things simply don't feel real—until it's too late.

I rolled over to snap on the lamp—I had some confused idea of trying to get the attention of the police car parked outside—as Chris sprang out of the armoire.

"Wait," I cried. "Wait, don't do this!" Neither original nor useful.

He was laughing, and it was one of the most terrifying things I'd ever seen. "I can't fucking believe it," he said in perfectly normal tones. "I've been trying and trying to find you, and you *summoned* me."

I blinked at him, trying to understand.

Horrified realization dawned.

The finding spell. This is the problem with being out of practice. I had apparently messed up the spell. I had located Chris, all right, and then I'd brought him straight to *me*.

"See?" he said. "There *is* a connection."

I stared. The upper half of his face was still red from the pepper spray. Following my gaze, he sobered and put a hand up self-consciously. "That little bitch tried to pepper-spray me. Luckily, she mostly missed. Turns out I'm allergic to it. She could have killed me."

Clearly, the irony was lost on him.

I knew I should keep him talking—except, what was the point of keeping him talking if nobody was coming to rescue me? And nobody was coming to rescue me. The police would not try to break in based on my turning on my bedroom light. I didn't see how I could get to a phone before he grabbed me. But then again, he didn't seem to have a weapon...

I said, mostly because I needed to say something, "I don't understand why you're doing this."

"Somebody has to. For God's sake. The situation is only getting worse. If you read history, you can see the trajectory.

Half of you don't even hide it anymore. You're right out there on TV, performing your rituals and celebrating your Sabbats."

"You're talking about Wicca. That's not even the same thing."

"It's *all* the same thing."

Right. Now I understood something else. Why he had seemed to focus on Wiccans rather than Witches. Witches were more difficult prey. Harder to find, harder to catch, harder to kill. It was that simple.

Belatedly, I started inching toward the bedroom door. If I could get downstairs to the postern, I could vanish within a couple of seconds. Unless he was hanging on to me. Out of shape though I was, I thought I could guarantee he would not.

Reading my intention correctly, Chris grinned and moved to cut me off from the doorway, matching my little shuffling steps, mimicking my distracted expression.

The mockery did it—snapped me out of my paralysis, angered me. I said, "Were you hunting me at Misdirections?"

He got a funny look on his face. "No. I wasn't. I didn't even realize what you were—and what your friends were—until I noticed your jewelry at your shop. The bracelets, the amulet, right there in the open where anyone could see. I even thought for a couple of minutes that maybe it was a sign. A sign for me to stop. That if we were fated... But we aren't. That wasn't the sign."

"And then you followed me to Paris and tried to drown me."

"Huh? I've never been to Paris." He seemed honestly surprised.

It surprised me too. I'd taken it for granted that whoever had pushed me into the Seine was part of the same conspiracy, but it turned out there was no conspiracy. There was only one psycho on a mission.

It seemed even Ralph had been telling the truth.

"What happens now?" I asked.

"Now? Now you'll try to run, and I'll hit you with my hammer." He drew a perfectly ordinary-looking hammer out of his jacket pocket. "Or we can do it the more civilized way. You hand over your athame, we sit down and share a bottle of…"

He was still talking, but I didn't hear what he said. I stared at the hammer, stared at Chris.

I murmured, "*Turn around, knock him—*"

Before I could finish the spell, Chris hurled the hammer at my head. The speed and vicious accuracy of that move were totally unexpected. Not his first witch murder, after all.

I ducked, barely in time, and the hammer hit the wall, denting it. At the same instant, Pyewacket, crouching atop the armoire, sprang down, hissing, claws extended, landing on Chris's head and shoulders.

Chris screamed, grabbed the spitting, wriggling cat, and hurled him against the armoire.

"*No!*"

Pye thumped against the doors, yowled, and went limp.

I chanted, "*Ejecerunt foras, removere illud de sphaera! Huius terminus—*"

"Sticks and stones may break my bones," Chris sneered, and tackled me.

This is the problem with theory versus practical application. When practicing spellcasting, the focus is on getting the spells right. In an actual fight for your life, it comes down to speed and aim.

We crashed through the open doorway and landed in the unlit hall. Chris punched me in the face, which immobilized me for precious seconds with shock and pain.

No one expects the Spanish Inquisition…

It wasn't that I wasn't trained in self-defense. I had trained since childhood. But it was months since I'd attended a class, and I was out of shape. I was also jet lagged, and I'd had a hella rough weekend. My reaction times were slow, my responses disorganized.

He let go of me, scrambled back on all fours to grab his hammer—and I jackknifed up and turned to run. He grabbed my leg, hurled me back from the top of the staircase, and I let the momentum carry me a few feet down the hall, away from him. I came down hard, the breath knocked out of my lungs and my twisted knee throbbing painfully.

I had the dim impression that a light went on downstairs. Had the cops in the patrol car been alerted by the sounds of our brawl? I stumbled up, limping, careened into the wall, kept going, and found myself heading straight into the dead end of the second guestroom.

As I staggered past the Louis XVI rococo mirror, I saw shadowy motion in its silvery depths.

"*Uncle*," I gasped.

"There is no *uncle* in this game," Chris said from right behind me. He was literally on my heels, and I tripped and went down as he swung his hammer again. It was a two-handed swing—he was dead-set on killing me that time—and the head of the hammer smashed into the mirror.

An explosion of glittering glass, burning my face and bare chest, and a blaze of white light that turned the scene in the hallway into a frozen negative.

Everything dark was bright. Everything bright was dark. I saw Chris sprawled on the floor, his hammer a few inches from his hand, as he blinked up at... Great-great-great-uncle Arnold.

Yes. Great-great-great-uncle Arnold was finally free of his prison.

He looked at Chris, looked at me, looked at Chris—and smiled.

It was a terrible smile. He pointed at Chris and said in an unnerving singsong,

"*Here we have a little worm*
Let us see him laugh and squirm
If we let him crawl away
Let his brain forget this day."

Chris began to shriek with laughter and writhe on the floor.

Great-great-great-uncle Arnold turned his attention to me. "Good evening, Nephew."

"Good evening, Uncle," I said faintly.

He opened his mouth…and I realized that someone was pounding up the staircase.

John shouted, "Cos? *Cosmo?*"

Great-great-great-uncle Arnold nodded his head graciously. "Another time perhaps."

He faded from sight as John rounded the corner, skidding to a stop at the sight of Chris shrieking with laughter and wriggling on the floor. His horrified gaze traveled to me, back against the wall, staring at him.

"Cos? You okay?" All at once his voice was easy, calm. He walked toward me, crunching glass underfoot, stepping past Chris. He kicked the hammer away and then reached his hand out to me. "All right, sweetheart?"

I took his hand, and he pulled me to my feet. "Are you okay? Did he hurt you?" He still sounded weirdly conversational.

I opened my mouth. No words came. "You want to tell me what happened?"

"Not really," I said.

John made a smothered sound and pulled me into his arms.

Chapter Twenty

The moon had faded and the sun was rising by the time John saw the last uniformed officers to the door.

Jinx was in the kitchen. I could hear the kettle whistling and the *chink* of pottery as she fixed tea.

"Seven lives left," I murmured to Pyewacket, stroking his silky fur. He was curled on my lap as I sat on the sofa in the sunken living room. "You have to be more careful."

He gave a squeaky little *mew*.

"Yeah, but I had it under control," I told him.

Pye sneezed, though it was probably supposed to be a snort.

I glanced up as John came down the steps. He still looked weary, grim, but there was something in his eyes I hadn't seen for what felt like a very long time. Warmth. Light. He took his place on the sofa beside me, tugging me over so that I could rest comfortably against his shoulder. Pye meowed in protest but chose not to move.

I closed my eyes, listening to the steady pound of John's heart beneath my ear.

"Thank you for coming," I whispered.

His response was quiet, wry. "I didn't do anything."

I nodded. "Yes. You did."

I jumped at the crash of pottery. John sighed.

He threw back his head, called, "Everything okay in there?"

"Got it," Jinx called back.

Pyewacket made a muttery sound and tried to make himself more comfortable.

"Still think this was a great idea?" John asked softly.

I smiled, closed my eyes again. "Yeah."

He kissed my forehead.

So many things I wanted, *needed*, to ask him. Not just about what would happen now with Ciara. Surely the murder charges would be dropped? Surely she would at least be able to get bail? But also, who at City Hall, in his opinion, might possibly be a spy for the SPMMR.

I had other questions too. Questions John would not be able to answer. Who had tried to kill Rex? Who had tried to drown me in Paris? Where in the Nine Gates of Hell had Great-great-great Uncle Arnold got to? How did Oliver know so many things about my private life that he shouldn't know—and whose side was he on?

And finally, most importantly, why had John—

"Here we go!" Jinx said brightly. The tea tray wobbled alarmingly as she carried it down the short flight of steps.

John hastily let go of me, rising to help her. I sat up, soothing Pye. John lowered the tray to the table.

"You should be in bed, Cos," Jinx said, taking the chair across from the sofa. "You look terrible. You're already getting a black eye."

I probably felt terrible too, but I was still pumped full of adrenaline. Not the adrenaline of fighting for my life. The adrenaline of John being near me. Of John taking his seat on the sofa once more, settling me against him. I smiled at him.

He didn't smile back, but his expression was still kind, still concerned. "Just be glad you don't have a broken nose," he said. Some of my happiness faded.

Jinx said, "It's a good thing I'm staying here for a couple of days. You're going to be stiff as a board in a few hours."

"Oh yeah," John said. "You'll be a great help to him."

"I will!"

"Stop," I said, and I wasn't kidding.

Jinx poured tea for the three of us, chattering all the while. "I still can't believe Valenti's stepbrother was the Witch Killer. This is going to be so terrible for her. What was he thinking? He could kill every witch in San Francisco?"

"Something like that," I said.

"What will happen to him?"

John said harshly, "He'll be convicted of three homicides and two attempted homicides, and they'll shut him up in a hospital for the criminally insane for the rest of his life. If I have anything to say about it."

No compassion there. But I wasn't going to argue. Chris had been raving when they'd finally loaded him into the ambulance and driven off into the night.

"Poor Valenti," Jinx said again. She shuddered. "Even so, I'm glad I'm not staying there tonight. Thank you guys for letting me stay here. Although with the Witch Killer locked up, I'm looking forward to going home and sleeping in my own bed again."

"How did you get on with my mother?" I asked curiously.

Jinx beamed. "I *love* her."

John choked on his tea.

When Jinx finally went up to bed and Pye had departed to lick his emotional wounds in private, John and I sat for a few minutes in silence on the sofa. He still had his arm around me, and I was grateful for that comfort.

I knew he probably wasn't going to stay. That though he clearly did care for me, he probably still did not—could not—forgive me. I knew that once he made his mind up, that was pretty much that. And he had decided that both me and our marriage were a mistake.

But somehow with his arm wrapped warmly around me, and his head leaning ever so slightly against mine, I was able to pretend that everything would be okay.

The grandfather clock tolled the hour in five slow, silvery chimes.

"Why did you come back here tonight?" I asked finally.

"Because it's killing me to be away from you."

He said it so calmly, so quietly, it took me a moment to realize the words were real.

I sat up. Stared at him. "But I thought…"

"Yes. I thought so too." He shook his head. "It doesn't seem to matter what I think. What I feel here is completely different." He touched my fist to his chest. "I know you say there's no love spell on me, but something happened. Something changed. The idea of living without you is…" He repeated, and his tone was pained, "It's killing me."

"John, couldn't we try again? It would be different now. It really would. And I promise—I'll swear on anything you like— that I'll never lie to you. Never use magic on you. Never…"

In the face of his silence, I slowed to a stop.

There were lines in his face I'd only seen once. When I'd nearly drowned in the Seine.

"I want to believe you. I even do believe you. In some ways."

"It's the truth."

When he didn't answer, I said, "Why *can't* you believe me? It wasn't all lies between us. Mostly, the important parts, were all truth. Why is it so hard to trust? Couldn't you at least give me the benefit of the doubt?"

He gave a slight shake of his head.

I said tentatively, "Is it because of what happened in Somalia?"

His face changed. For a second I saw the terrifying mask of the night he had discovered I was a witch. "What do you know about Somalia?" His voice didn't sound like his own.

"Nothing. Andi told me that Trace had confided in her about some things that happened during the war. She wondered—she said he wondered—if you had told me about it."

"No. Never. That's something I'm never going to talk about. Not with you. Not with anyone."

I didn't know what to say. I looked away. Nodded.

He said nothing.

I said, "I wasn't prying. It's just… I was hoping it might explain why you can't…forgive me."

He drew in a sharp breath and hauled me back into his arms. My face was buried against him, so I couldn't see or read his. I could barely breathe. He said against my ear, "It isn't… It's not something I can do." I felt his swallow. "But you're not… That's not about you. I do not equate you with that."

For some reason, it brought tears to my eyes. I shook my head, didn't try to speak.

He said in that same almost deathly quiet, urgent voice, "I do forgive you, Cos. I do love you. I don't know if I can—"

I had to breathe, and it came out in a shuddery sigh. I pulled away from him, wiped hastily at my face.

"Okay. I get it."

Which was the first lie I'd told him in a long time.

We didn't speak for what felt like hours. Then he said slowly, "In Paris, you said you were trying not to use magic. Not to live a magical life. Is that true?"

I said huskily, "Yes."

His breath hitched, and he leaned forward, turning my face to his. "I know this probably isn't fair to ask. But if you could do that, if you could commit to giving up magic—if you'll promise never to use witchcraft again— Could you make that compromise?" His eyes were fiercely intent.

It took me a moment to understand what he was saying, what he was asking. And I *wanted* to. I wanted to do anything that would make him love me again. I would gladly have given him anything within my power.

But that was not within my power. That was no compromise. He was asking me to give up who I was.

I opened my mouth, saw the hope in his eyes, that he believed he had found the way for us.

It took all my strength to shake my head. "No."

John sank back, the light dying out of his face.

"That's…too much."

"That's what I thought." He didn't sound angry or bitter. Just tired.

I put my hands on his shoulders, forcing him to look at me.

"It isn't fair, John. It's one thing if I choose to live a mortal life. If I choose not to use my…abilities. It's another for you to make it a condition. That's not a compromise. What you're saying is you can't accept me as I am, don't want me if I can't become the person you say I should be."

His lips parted, but I knew I had to finish, or I'd never have the courage to get the words out. "You're asking me to change my very nature, and the thing is, I feel so much for you, I want to agree. Even though I know it's not right, I still want to promise anything you want if it will make you love me again."

No gold glints in John's eyes now. They were dark as night.

I steadied my voice. "But if I agree, it will be a lie. However much I tried, I think I would eventually break my promise, and one thing I won't do ever again is lie to you." I managed a tremulous smile. "I did learn that lesson."

John nodded curtly, looked away. A muscle moved in his jaw.

I let out a shaky breath. I can't say I felt better for having rejected his "compromise." In fact, my heart was breaking. The crucial difference between John and me was he had always been ready to walk away from a bad deal. Whereas it was tearing me apart to tell him no. To forever end it between us. But what he was asking *was* wrong, and while I was no expert at relationships, I knew enough to know that if John couldn't love me as I was, there was no chance of saving our marriage anyway.

The grandfather clocked tick-tocked loud, long minutes into that empty silence.

John turned to me. He said gruffly, "Could you at least promise to *try* not to use magic as a first option?"

I stared, afraid to hope that he was saying what I so desperately longed to hear. "Yes," I whispered. "Of course, I promise. I *swear*. I'll only use magic as a last resort." I added honestly, "Or if I forget."

His mouth twisted, he shook his head, and to my startled and abject relief, pulled me into his arms. "You're wrong about not wanting you—not loving you—as you are. It scares me how much I care. I don't think it's possible for me *not* to love you."

Much later, when we were lying upstairs in the brass four-poster, warmly wrapped in each other's arms, basking in the Happily Ever Afterglow, he said, "Did you really tell Chief Morrisey's wife you're pregnant?"

"Mm-hmm…"

John snorted, brushed a strand of hair from my forehead. He said suddenly, "You're not, are you?"

I laughed, then said thoughtfully, "I don't think so."

He half sat up. "Y-you don't *think* so? You mean it's possible?"

"I don't think so."

"You're not sure?"

I lifted a shoulder. "There are a few old legends about witch kings bearing children. They're probably metaphors, don't you think?"

"*Probably?*"

"Probably."

"You don't *know*?"

"Well, I *think* I know."

"Let me see if I understand this. Are you saying— You're saying a male witch can become pregnant?"

"I've never known it to happen."

He slowly lowered himself to the mattress. Drew me to him as cautiously as if I were a ticking time bomb.

I said mildly, "Would it be so terrible if I were carrying your child?"

"You're kidding, right? Would it be so terrible if my *husband* were carrying my child?" And yet he sounded more bemused than outraged.

I smiled blandly. "You have to admit it would be the détente to end all détentes: the child of the witch king and a witch hunter."

John's gulp was so loud, Pyewacket, curled in his favorite outpost on the window seat, raised his head.

John studied my face. He said slowly, dangerously, "You little... You're yanking my chain, aren't you?"

I laughed. "Am I? Probably."

He put his hand around my throat and squeezed, but lightly, teasingly. "I don't know what to do with you."

I said, "Oh, I think you have *some* idea what to do with me..."

Author Notes

Thank you so much to Keren Reed for getting the hurly burly done and all the battles won. And thank you to the SO. YES, YOU DO STILL HAVE A WIFE.

Thank you in advance to Kale Williams for what I know will be a terrific audiobook—CAN'T WAIT FOR YOU TO READ ALL THAT LATIN IN FRENCH ACCENTS AGAIN.

Thank you to my patrons for keeping the cauldron boiling and the home fires burning.

And finally, thank YOU, dear readers, for buying this book. If you enjoyed it, please consider leaving a review.

About the Author

Author of over sixty titles of classic Male/Male fiction featuring twisty mystery, kickass adventure, and unapologetic man-on-man romance, JOSH LANYON'S work has been translated into twelve languages. Her FBI thriller *Fair Game* was the first Male/Male title to be published by Harlequin Mondadori, then the largest romance publisher in Italy. *Stranger on the Shore* (Harper Collins Italia) was the first M/M title to be published in print. In 2016 *Fatal Shadows* placed #5 in Japan's annual Boy Love novel list (the first and only title by a foreign author to place on the list). The Adrien English series was awarded the All Time Favorite Couple by the Goodreads M/M Romance Group. In 2019, *Fatal Shadows* became the first LGBTQ mobile game created by Moments: Choose Your Story.

She is an Eppie Award winner, a four-time Lambda Literary Award finalist (twice for Gay Mystery), an Edgar nominee, and the first ever recipient of the Goodreads All Time Favorite M/M Author award.

Josh is married and lives in Southern California.

Find other Josh Lanyon titles at www.joshlanyon.com, and follow her on Twitter, Facebook, Goodreads, Instagram and Tumblr.

For extras and other exclusives, please join Josh on Patreon at https://www.patreon.com/joshlanyon.

Also By Josh Lanyon

NOVELS

The ADRIEN ENGLISH Mysteries
Fatal Shadows • A Dangerous Thing • The Hell You Say
Death of a Pirate King • The Dark Tide
So This is Christmas • Stranger Things Have Happened

The HOLMES & MORIARITY Mysteries
Somebody Killed His Editor • All She Wrote
The Boy with the Painful Tattoo • In Other Words...Murder

The ALL'S FAIR Series
Fair Game • Fair Play • Fair Chance

The ART OF MURDER Series
The Mermaid Murders •The Monet Murders
The Magician Murders • The Monuments Men Murders

OTHER NOVELS

The Ghost Wore Yellow Socks
Mexican Heat (with Laura Baumbach)
Strange Fortune • Come Unto These Yellow Sands
This Rough Magic • Stranger on the Shore • Winter Kill
Murder in Pastel • Jefferson Blythe, Esquire
The Curse of the Blue Scarab • Murder Takes the High Road
Séance on a Summer's Night
The Ghost Had an Early Check-Out

NOVELLAS

The DANGEROUS GROUND Series
Dangerous Ground • Old Poison • Blood Heat
Dead Run • Kick Start

The I SPY Series
I Spy Something Bloody • I Spy Something Wicked
I Spy Something Christmas

The IN A DARK WOOD Series
In a Dark Wood • The Parting Glass

The DARK HORSE Series
The Dark Horse • The White Knight

The DOYLE & SPAIN Series
Snowball in Hell

The HAUNTED HEART Series
Haunted Heart Winter

The XOXO FILES Series
Mummie Dearest

OTHER NOVELLAS

Cards on the Table • The Dark Farewell
The Darkling Thrush • The Dickens with Love
Don't Look Back • A Ghost of a Chance
Lovers and Other Strangers • Out of the Blue
A Vintage Affair • Lone Star (in Men Under the Mistletoe)
Green Glass Beads (in Irregulars)
Blood Red Butterfly • Everything I Know
Baby, It's Cold • A Case of Christmas
Murder Between the Pages • Slay Ride